"That pair is romantic," Whitney went on, "but they're romantic in a technically precise sort of way."

"You mean, like this," replied Brent, nestling his arm into the curve of her waist and sweeping her completely off her sneakered feet, his eyes gazing deeply into hers.

"Y-yes," she stammered, her knees suddenly weak and wobbly. Pausing long enough against the barre to catch her breath as well as her runaway emotions, she corrected herself again. "I mean *no*. You can't compare us to that couple, Brent. What they've perfected . . ."

"Is romance—both on the ice and off," Brent finished for her. "And we haven't had much of a chance to practice that ourselves, have we?" he added with a mischievous grin.

Whitney felt the color rise in her cheeks. What did Brent think—that love was something you practiced like a complicated lift until you finally got it right?

"Can't we at least give it a try?" Brent pleaded.

The SILVER SKATES Series
by Barbara J. Mumma
Published by Fawcett Girls Only Books:

BREAKING THE ICE (#1)

Other titles in the Girls Only series available upon request

SILVER SKATES   2

Winner's Waltz

Barbara J. Mumma

FAWCETT GIRLS ONLY • NEW YORK

RLI: $\dfrac{\text{VL 6 \& up}}{\text{IL 7 \& up}}$

A Fawcett Girls Only Book
Published by Ballantine Books
Copyright © 1988 by Cloverdale Press, Inc.

Library of Congress Catalog Card Number: 88-91165

ISBN 0-449-13460-1

Manufactured in the United States of America

First Edition: November 1988

Cover photo by Roy Blakey

For Jennifer Sayres:
Because if I could pick my relatives, I'd pick you.

One

Trusting Brent Marks, her ice dancing partner, was a *big* mistake, fumed Whitney Backman as she skidded across the ice on her backside for the fourth time that day.

Scrambling to her feet, she didn't even bother to sweep the frost from her black skating skirt before propelling herself furiously toward her tall, redheaded partner.

"And where were you *that* time?" she said, her hands poised primly on her slender hips. "Don't try to tell me that you were lost in your thoughts. We both know you've never *had* any."

Flushed with exertion and anger, Brent drew his lips into a thin line. "Oh, believe me, Whitney— I've had a few. And if you could read my mind right *now*, you'd know just what a spoiled, selfish little southern prima donna I think you are."

Tossing her dark blond, shoulder-length hair, Whitney leaned forward until she was nearly nose-to-nose with her handsome partner, ready with a scathing comeback.

"If you two don't stop that bickering right now, you'll *both* be doing some reading—of the worst scores ever awarded in the history of the Eastern Championships." Crumpling his used Styrofoam coffee cup in one huge hand, Coach Gregory Mastroni glared at the duo locked in mortal combat at the far end of the rink. "Now take it from the top of the waltz sequence."

"He's right, you know," murmured Brent, taking his position mid-ice as emphatically as a soldier planting his flag on enemy territory. "If you don't start watching your feet we could end up in third place—just like we did at Regionals."

"If I don't start watching *my* feet!" As Whitney's usually soft, accented voice rose from a whisper to a shriek, she saw Gregory Mastroni's bushy eyebrows arch in anger and surprise.

Smiling demurely at her coach, she struck her dramatic opening pose, continuing her ongoing tirade under her breath.

"My feet are not the problem and you know it! Skating around those size-eleven banana boats of yours is like skating through an obstacle course! And your hands are as cold as an Eskimo's."

Brent slipped his arm around her stiffened waist. "Well, maybe it's got something to do with all this *blubber* I've been hauling around for the last six years."

Before Whitney had a chance to reply the first swirling notes of their contemporary waltz selection filled the massive arena.

It wasn't that she didn't like the music that had become so much a part of their free-dance routine. Skating to instrumental renditions of Beatles classics had become their trademark, just as the theme from Bolero was that of the renowned Olympic Gold Medalists Jane Torvill and Christopher Dean.

Balancing on the very tip of her toe pick, Whitney watched as Brent made his approach, swirling seductively around her on his black skates as if to tempt her into motion. Theirs had been an "arranged" partnership—a marriage of their respective builds, skating styles, and looks. Both of them born in Atlanta, drawn to the same rink, Brent and Whitney had grown together artistically without outgrowing each other physically. What more could they ask for?

Yet, as they made their way around the perimeter of the enormous rink, punctuating each musical beat with a daring lean or dazzling turn, it seemed to Whitney that a great many aspects of their often stormy relationship could have been improved.

Brent, for instance, could have lost his voice, which would reduce the bickering that came so naturally to them by at least half. And he could have lost his infuriating tendency to guide her too near the boards, reducing the probability of injury. And most of all, Brent could have kept his head on that hot July night four months ago when he had begun to see her as something more than just a partner. Ever since the team of Backman and Marks had been at each other's throats.

Yet as haunting refrains of "Something" echoed in the huge Olympic arena, Whitney couldn't help but give herself over to the music—and to the guidance of her skillful partner.

"Something in the way you move," Brent panted in time to the lilting, familiar tune, "reminds me of a charging rhino."

"Just get on with it, all right?"

Whitney cringed slightly as Brent lifted her up over the ice, leading her gently but firmly into a series of twists. She could feel his body stiffen, as if repelled by the hand she rested on his shoulder, the cheek she pressed to his chest.

Then they began the most challenging of their maneuvers, a move in which Brent stepped over Whitney's prone, spinning body, then pulled her back to her feet in one smooth motion.

As Whitney spiraled around her partner's feet, something seemed unbalanced. She held out her hand for Brent to bring her back up again.

Suddenly, instead of feeling the ice surface under her feet, Whitney felt it tearing at her side.

"Ouch," she said, flinching as the snow stung her skin. She struggled to pull herself upright. "Nice catch, Brent! Right out of the USFSA rule book. Let's see, which number was that? Three-twenty-four? How to break your partner's leg?"

"Whitney!" scolded Gregory Mastroni from the

barrier. He was standing beside a tall, elderly woman who was watching the developing melee with an expressionless face.

"Well, I'm getting sick of this," complained Whitney, brushing the back of her black skating skirt violently. "Brent throws great, but he couldn't catch a cold in a rainstorm. And he certainly can't seem to catch *me*."

Whitney expected Gregory Mastroni to tell her once again that any bickering she did was to be done on her time, not his. Instead, he bent his head toward the slight, gray-haired woman who was whispering intently in his ear.

"Who is that?" Whitney wondered aloud. She wasn't accustomed to performing for an audience during her private lessons.

"You really don't know?" Brent answered, busying himself with the elastic strap that kept his skating pants firmly attached to the boots of his skates.

Coach Mastroni cleared his throat violently to catch his students' attention. "It has been pointed out to me that this particular fall may not have been the fault of the catcher," he said. "As a matter of fact, it seems that *you*, Whitney, may have been out of position on that move."

Mr. Mastroni gave the woman beside him a nudge and she began to speak slowly and haltingly in heavily accented English.

"I merely suggest that perhaps if the young woman had not fallen off of her edge, she would have extended herself naturally to within her partner's reach."

Whitney frowned and turned back to her waiting partner. "So what does she know?" she said resentfully.

Brent raised his eyebrows. "After two national champions and a slew of coaching successes, she probably knows a lot."

Peeking over Brent's broad shoulder, Whitney took in the visitor, from the top of her neat, gray-blond chignon to the tip of her fragile-looking hands.

Whitney's curiosity was getting the better of her. "So who *is* she? And who is that with her?"

Scanning the dimly lit arena seats, Brent's eyes lit on a girl of about their own age, whose wavy, honey-colored hair shimmered past her shoulders like sheaves of sun-ripened wheat.

"Does the name Michaela Frankel mean anything to you?" he asked, beaming.

"Well of course it does. She's the East German national ice dance champion with the partner—"

"Whom she left behind in East Germany when she defected to the United States with her aunt, Elena Ott," Brent finished. He was standing midice with a silly smile on his face.

The light dawned. "Oh," Whitney said finally. "But what are they doing here in Lake Placid?"

"That I don't know," Brent answered with a shrug. "But I have a feeling we're about to find out."

At the rail, Gregory Mastroni and Elena Ott were continuing their hushed discussion. Suddenly, the skating school director raised his eyes.

"Whitney, Brent—could we see your Kilian, please? Just four patterns—twice around the rink."

Whitney and Brent groaned simultaneously. "He's only seen us do that stupid dance three thousand times in the last three months," Whitney complained.

"Cheer up," said Brent. "You can think of it as a chance to spend another few moments of bliss in my arms."

Jabbing her toe pick into the ice violently enough to send a shower of snow onto her teasing partner's skate, Whitney settled uncomfortably into Brent's outstretched arms, her back ramrod straight.

The Kilian was a compulsory set pattern dance, and the two of them had performed it in competition countless times. But right now Whitney couldn't help feeling that the relatively simple fourteen-step dance was turning out more like a frenzied game of "I'll trip you before you trip me."

They hadn't even managed one complete circuit of the ice before Coach Mastroni signaled them in.

"Here is someone I think you should meet," he said tersely, waving his hand toward the spectator. "Elena Ott, Whitney Backman and Brent Marks. Believe me, they're better than they look."

"I'm pleased to meet you," offered Whitney, extending her hand. The elderly skater did not return the gesture.

"I am sure our association will be a very long and prosperous one," she said in a formal tone.

Whitney and Brent glanced at each other, confused. Association? Was she at the Lake Placid school in some official capacity?

"I think that what Miss Ott is saying is that she looks forward to getting to know you," explained Gregory Mastroni. "And that she is pleased to take over for me temporarily as your coach."

"Coach? But you're our coach," Whitney blurted, momentarily forgetting all of her genteel southern manners. "We came to the Lake Placid Skating School with the understanding that you would be training us."

"No offense," Brent added with a quick look toward the pretty girl watching the proceedings intently from the arena seats.

"Right—no slight intended," Whitney echoed. "But with a major competition coming up in just two weeks ..."

"And considering that Whitney's timing has been a little off in the last few months ..." Brent's voice trailed off.

"You've both been under a lot of pressure lately," Gregory Mastroni shifted uncomfortably in his weather-beaten leather jacket. "But I think that the arrangement will be better for you."

Again Whitney and Brent turned to each other in bewilderment.

"Besides," their coach continued, "you will benefit from the advice of someone in your own field. Especially now that there are problems."

Whitney sighed heavily. If it weren't for Brent and his stupid romantic ideas, there wouldn't *be* any problems.

"But this is all so—sudden," she said. And frightening, she added to herself.

"Well, you'll have to get used to it," declared

Coach Mastroni, obviously growing impatient. Without another word, he gave the elderly woman a pat on the back and left the ice, heading toward the bleak, windowless rink office.

"So what are we supposed to do?" called Whitney.

"First, you'll be here tomorrow at your regularly scheduled time," he called, never missing a beat. "Second, you're going to trust me." He paused at the office door. "Do you think you can handle that?"

Whitney nodded numbly. How could she trust a man who had just passed her and Brent off to a complete stranger like a box of unwanted kittens?

Nodding to Elena Ott, she snatched up the rubber skate guards she had left on the barrier and stomped off down the padded walkway. "Hey, wait up," Brent called after her, but Whitney didn't even glance back over her shoulder. Today had been an absolute disaster, and she wanted to be left alone—maybe forever.

Two

　　"Eee-aaagh!" In one swift movement, Whitney jumped up from the cluttered floor of her third-floor room and onto a wobbly, antique wooden chair.

　　"Now if only you could move like that *on* the ice...." commented her roommate, Katie Arden, in obvious amusement.

　　"Yeah. Then you could even be a singles skater," finished Cyndi Scott, pouring the last of a package of M&M's into her palm. "And it'd be bye-bye Brent Marks and bye-bye troubles—forever."

　　"If you don't tell me what these disgusting things are, it'll be bye-bye roommates forever!" Whitney shrieked. She pointed to the two slimy creatures lolling amid the dried flowers on top of her dresser.

"Now *what* are they? And what are they doing in *here*?"

Cyndi made her way to the dresser and cradled one of the creatures in her hand. "For Pete's sake, Whitney, keep your voice down. Can't you see you're scaring the poor things?"

"Oh, baloney. There's no way I can scare them half as much as they scare me." Whitney peered down in horror as Cyndi stroked the animal gently with her index finger. "I don't even know if they bite."

Claire Glass, engrossed in her history assignment, barely lifted her eyes from the page she was reading. "They're newts. Small amphibians that can be distinguished from the terrestrial forms of life by their compressed, fishlike tails. And, of course, by the fact that they are oviparous."

"That means they don't bite, right?" persisted Whitney.

"It means that they lay eggs," answered Claire calmly.

"Well, they'd better not be laying any eggs in this room," warned Whitney. "Does everybody hear me?"

"The way you're carrying on, they'll hear you in Canada," commented Cyndi, placing one of the small amphibians squarely on Katie's head.

"Okay, okay," Whitney said, clambering down from her perch. "I can tell when I've been out-numbered." She regarded the crawling lizards with disdain. "But that doesn't mean I'm feeding these things whatever they eat. And they'd better not make a newt condominium out of *my* dresser. Whose creatures are these, anyway?"

Her roommates looked at each other and burst into laughter.

"They're yours," choked Cyndi, her apple-round cheeks flushed a deep pink.

"What?" Whitney's mouth dropped open.

"They're yours," Cyndi repeated gleefully.

"Is this some kind of a sick Yankee joke?" Whitney said, hands on hips. "Because if it is, it *isn't* very funny."

"It's no joke, Whitney," Katie replied. "The newts *are* yours. And mine and Tom's and Brent's."

"Two full sets of parents," chortled Cyndi.

Whitney was relieved. In a pinch, the newts could always be moved, lock, stock, and seaweed, from the girls' dormitory—Halloran House—to the Acton Inn, where the male students of the Lake Placid Skating School were housed. Considering the appalling conditions under which most boys were content to live, it would be like moving from one mud hole to another for the newts.

"They're *all* of ours, really," Katie corrected. "But since I'm the one who actually *caught* them with an empty peanut butter jar, I thought it might be fun to keep them here. Not just as scientific specimens but as pets. Especially since I almost ruined my best pair of jeans mucking around in that stupid mill pond."

"I had a pet once," Cyndi said. "A hamster."

"I have a kid brother," added Claire.

"Scientific specimens? Oh, for crying out loud." Whitney clapped her hand to her forehead "So *that's* what all this is about. That silly biology project we were all supposed to do together." She closed her eyes. "Okay, I remember Mr. Swayze giving us a paper to write. And I remember him telling us to research it carefully. But I don't remember him asking us to start our own newt ranch."

"Two newts don't exactly make a *ranch*, Whitney." Katie's voice crackled with irritation.

"Depends how long you leave them alone," commented Claire from behind her history textbook.

"Look, Whitney, do I have to remind you that this paper is worth forty percent of our final grade?" said Katie with a frown. "All four of us missed classes because of our crazy skating schedules, and we can really use the extra credit. The only way we're going to get it is to do a bang-up report on the life cycle of the northern pond newt."

Whitney sighed deeply. "All right. I get the picture. When is this big project due again?"

"In two weeks—three days after the Eastern competitions."

"Oh, great," Whitney said with a groan. "And when are we supposed to begin this monumental study?"

Katie grinned. "In about an hour."

"Tonight!" said Whitney, flinging herself onto Katie's lower bunk. "I just spent the entire afternoon fighting with Brent, and I'd rather do *anything* than see that creep right now. Count me out!" Too late, she realized that her voice was rising higher and higher.

There was a knock at the marred wooden door.

"You girls!" said a familiar voice. "Making an

old lady walk up three flights of stairs to see what all this noise is about! Now are you going to let me in or not?"

"Look what all of your yelling got us, Whitney—a visit from Mrs. McGregor," said Cyndi in disgust. Leaping to her feet, she began to scout the room for contraband. She yanked open her closet door and began to fling all of the junk food she had collected over the past several days into it: candy bars, snack cakes, corn chips, and yogurt-covered raisins. As far as the housemother was concerned, they were all "mouse magnets"—and strictly taboo in the Victorian house that served as their dorm.

"The *newts*!" Claire was standing near the door, frantically waving her arms.

Grabbing the closest item in which to contain the creatures—one of Cyndi's knee socks—Katie attempted to stuff the wriggling amphibians inside.

Selma McGregor was obviously growing impatient. "Come on now, open up. The longer I knock, the later your dinner."

"I'm putting on my robe, Mrs. M," sang Claire. "I'll be right there. The dresser!" she hissed in Katie's direction.

Allowing Katie just enough time to sweep the newts into Whitney's top dresser drawer and slam it shut, Claire opened the door to the cramped third-floor suite, smiling her most innocent smile.

"Well, it's about time!" huffed the housemother, wiping her forehead with the linen handkerchief she pulled from the overstuffed bosom of her housedress. "A person could catch their death waiting around in that drafty old hallway! Especially after working up a sweat on those terrible stairs. *Three* flights! Why, you girls must make me out to be a mountain goat the way you force me up and down, up and down, every time you get to fussing. Now what's going on here?"

"Nothing, Mrs. McGregor." Sung out simultaneously, the girls' answer sounded very suspicious.

Mrs. McGregor looked doubtful. "Are you sure about that? I could swear—"

"Absolutely," Whitney broke in smoothly and her roommates nodded in agreement.

"All right, I'll be off to the kitchen," said the white-haired housekeeper, whirling on the heel of her orthopedic shoe. "My hearing must not be what it used to be, I guess."

Claire shut the door behind the still-muttering Mrs. McGregor as quietly as she could.

"Her hearing isn't what it *used* to be? She's got to be kidding," scoffed Cyndi, rescuing the snacks she had hidden from the chaos of her closet floor. "That woman could hear a candy wrapper rip at forty paces."

"Never mind that—just get those disgusting creatures out of my drawer!" Whitney's anger was still smoldering fiercely.

Katie began to rummage obediently through her roommate's collection of silk scarves and delicate gauze blouses. "Okay, okay," she said, putting first one, then another squirming newt from the neatly arranged drawer and depositing them gently onto her green floral bedspread. "See? No damage done."

Whitney shuddered.

"Whitney, it's time to go," Katie said, straightening up. "Come on, it's almost time to meet Brent and Tom." She propelled Whitney toward the door.

"Where *are* they?" asked Whitney impatiently, tapping the library table for emphasis.

The walk from Halloran House to Lake Placid High had been unnervingly silent, as though the anger that Whitney had brought home from the rink had met the upstate November chill head-on.

"Look," replied Katie, "What's your problem, anyway? Your face was as long as a coast-to-coast train trip from the minute you walked into the suite this afternoon."

Whitney pulled her fingers through her shiny blond hair. "The problem is if Brent and Tom don't get here soon, somebody else is going to take over the other half of this table. Then we won't have any place to work on this stupid paper. That would suit me just fine, I might add."

"Whew!" Katie said aloud, forgetting for the moment where she was. The librarian threw her a withering glance.

"Look, Whitney. I'm not your mother or your coach or the Lake Placid Skating School gestapo. I'm trying to help you, but I can't unless you tell me what happened at the rink today. Was Coach Mastroni on your back? Are you nervous about Easterns? Did you do one too many Backman Butt Slides and injure your brain? *What?*"

"All right, all right." As annoyed as she was by

her roommate's reference to her recent tendency to land anywhere other than on her feet, Whitney knew it would be easier to pull an old slipper out of a terrier's teeth than it would be to pull Katie off of the subject. "The answer is yes to all your questions. Yes, Coach Mastroni has been a real tyrant. Yes, I'm scared about Easterns, especially after our lousy performance at Regionals. And yes, I had more than a few wipeouts today. But that's just the tip of the iceberg." She twisted her face into a worried grimace and poured out the whole story—from her ongoing problems with Brent to her most recently acquired difficulty: a new coach.

"Elena Ott—here in Lake Placid? I can't believe it." Katie tapped the bridge of her nose pensively. "Her defection was in all the magazines."

"And now she's here to give us—me—the works," said Whitney with a sigh. "The works." Quickly she filled her roommate in on what had happened during the practice session.

"Changing coaches might be good for you two," Katie said slowly. "Elena Ott was world champion in ice dancing at least once...."

"Twice," said Whitney dismally.

"And she's coached nearly every world-class ice dance couple the East Germans have had to offer for at least twenty years—including last years's world champions, Licht and ... and ..."

"Frankel," sighed Whitney, staring blankly at the tabletop as though it were a crystal ball in which was mapped out her entire dismal future. "*Michaela* Frankel. Elena Ott's niece—and traveling companion."

Katie gasped. "Michaela Frankel is *here*? Without her partner?"

"Oh, she's here, all right—but something tells me she doesn't intend to be skating by herself for long."

Katie raised her eyebrows. "Are you trying to tell me that Michaela Frankel—a world champion—is here in Lake Placid to look for a new partner?"

The idea did seem farfetched. All of the ice dancers who had been invited to the Lake Placid Skating School had been accepted in pairs. It was hard to believe that Gregory Mastroni would allow an unattached skater to throw everything off. Still, Whitney remained adamant.

"Think about it, Katie. What *else* could she want? She left Andy Licht behind in East Germany. And now that the Olympics are only a short ways down the road, she's *got* to be scouting for a replacement." Whitney tapped the tabletop again with the tips of her perfectly manicured nails. "I mean, an Olympic ice dance contender wouldn't defect to begin a singles career, would she?"

Suddenly Brent was smiling down at Whitney from his six-foot height. "Hi there," he said, smoothing his curly red hair. He pulled out a chair across from her. Whitney looked away.

"Where have you guys been?" demanded Katie, her green eyes locked in mortal combat with exact replicas of her own—her twin brother's. "You knew we were supposed to meet here ..."

"Half an hour ago. I know, I know." Tom Arden buried his face in the arm of his sweater in mock repentance. "We beg your forgiveness. Now let's get on with this newt thing before we all die of boredom."

"Or embarrassment," said Brent, pulling his library copy of *The Newts of North America* out of the front of his orange satin baseball jacket.

"Okay then," began Katie, pulling three thick scientific volumes out of her book bag and slapping them on the table. "Everybody else, take your pick."

"You're kidding, right?" said Whitney. "Katie, *you* have already outlined the whole paper. You and I are stuck with the newts. And because Brent here is all thumbs—a condition to which I can attest—*we* are also stuck with all the typing. Why should we have to do the reading, too?"

"That's Whitney for you," said Brent. "Always looking for the easy way out. 'Why should I have to land on my feet when you can just catch me instead, Brent? Why should I have to make my turns match yours when you can make yours match mine? Why should I have to do *any* work when Brent can do it for me?'"

Katie's mouth dropped in astonishment. "Look," she began. "We're at the *library* now, not the rink. . . ."

"Or a boxing ring," added Tom with a quiet chuckle. Casting her brother a warning glance, Katie continued.

"The point is, if we can keep this project *off* the ice and think of working together as friends . . ."

"Friends?" The expression on Brent's handsome face was difficult to read. Although his lips were

twisted into a slight sneer, his eyes seemed full of pain.

Embarrassed, Whitney glanced nervously toward the end of the table where the twins were sitting, wide-eyed. What would they think? Brent sounded as angry as she still felt. At least Tom and Katie hadn't heard the little speech that Brent had delivered during their single, ill-fated date. *We could be so much more than partners, Whitney, or friends. I'm not afraid to admit it.*

Whitney leaned across the table toward her partner.

"The fact is, Mr. Marks," she hissed, "*friend* seems to be the only position available at this time. You can take it or leave it. The decision is entirely up to you."

"No problem," Brent declared, yanking the satin jacket from the back of his chair. "I'll leave." Tucking his book under one strong arm, he glanced at Tom. "Are you coming or what?"

Tom shrugged helplessly, then grinned nervously at his sister. "No newts is good newts, I guess," he offered lamely, scrambling awkwardly to his feet.

Katie leaned back in her chair, her arms folded in frustration. "That's just great. Two weeks to write this paper and off you go, abandoning us."

"It's not *you* I'm abandoning, Katie," Brent said quietly, guiding Tom hurriedly toward the library door.

Katie waited until the boys had made their escape to confront her furious roommate.

"Look, Whitney, I don't want to be nosy or

anything, but would you *please* give me some clue as to what that was all about? Tom and I have been skating together forever, and we've seen plenty of major squabbles. I might be able to help."

Help? Slinging her copy of *Amphibious Life* into her book bag, Whitney pushed herself away from the table. "Katie, you know perfectly well that Brent and I haven't been getting along lately. And you still insisted that we all get together just like one big, happy family." Hoisting the bag across her shoulders, Whitney leaned angrily toward her roommate. "I think you've helped enough for any one day." With that she turned and made her way quickly through the maze of tables, carts of books, and clusters of students that stood between her and the library door. All she wanted right now was to be left alone.

Three

"*At least* those newts are quiet," said Claire, adding a handful of soft, creamy mousse to her shoulder-length brown hair. "They aren't much fuss as pets go, and they certainly don't eat much." Bending at the waist, Claire brushed her hair vigorously, then stood and allowed it to fall freely around her angular face. "I think I'm getting attached to the little buggers."

"Well, I wouldn't get *too* attached if I were you," warned Whitney, launching her tiny five-foot frame onto her comfortable upper bunk. "For one thing, they'll probably freeze to death in this icebox of a room." Wrapping herself like a mummy in the heavy folds of her thick, green bedspread, she shivered dramatically. "For another thing, there simply isn't enough room in this suite for them and us...."

"And your 3,476 scarves," added Katie with a frown.

Suddenly a voice rose out of the third-floor hallway. "Either *she* goes or I go—and that's the end of it!"

"What was that?" asked Katie, looking at her roommates wide-eyed.

"This place is really strange sometimes," said Cyndi, calmly doing a few deep knee bends. "Too many girls in too little space. Sooner or later you're bound to start hearing things."

"It's Shelby Lang!" whispered Claire, her ear pressed firmly against the door. "She's talking to Mrs. McGregor. And maybe somebody else, but I can't tell who."

"Oooh," crooned Whitney, her blue eyes round with shock. "I can't believe that anybody could use that tone of voice with Mrs. M and get away with it. Even Shelby."

A true competitor both on and off the ice, Shelby Lang had earned a considerable reputation in the three months she had spent in Lake Placid, both as a singles skater of great promise and as an impossible housemate. The girls often snickered that it was no wonder that Shelby occupied the only single room at Halloran House, because it was the only room big enough to contain both Shelby and her ego.

"I can't believe this," scoffed Katie, slamming her journal shut with a bang. "For Pete's sake, Claire, what do you think you're doing?"

"Yeah, what *are* you doing?" said Cyndi, clapping the edge of a drinking glass to the oak door and pressing her ear to the bottom. "If you're going to eavesdrop this is the only way to go."

Katie shook her head. "Now I've seen everything."

"The point is that we *hear* everything," said Cyndi, fine-tuning the glass as if it were a high-powered transmitter.

Suddenly both girls jumped away from the door in amazement. The conversation outside had attained such volume that no eavesdropping techniques were necessary.

"Maybe one of us should go out there and see what's going on," said Whitney.

"Are you crazy? Shelby would rip us to pieces," warned Claire, who had already been cut once too often by the sharp-tongued girl's cruel barbs.

"Well, Shelby may think she's the queen of the dorm, but she can't stop us from using the bathroom." With a wink, Cyndi draped a towel casually over one arm and headed for the door. "I'll leave it open a crack," she said mischievously.

Katie rolled her eyes in disgust.

"Having a roommate is like picking up money from the street. There is no way you can know where it's been," Shelby was proclaiming in her haughty voice.

"Shelby Lang, you impertinent girl," scolded Mrs. McGregor. "This is a world-class skater you're talking about—not Typhoid Mary, for goodness' sake!"

Whitney did not have to see the scene to know that the housemother was now wringing her fleshy hands in frustration.

"Be that as it may, Mrs. McGregor," Shelby continued, "I was assigned a single room in September, and I intend to remain in it—alone—until June."

"Unless somebody kills her first," whispered Claire, leaning dangerously close to the opening to check Cyndi's progress down the hallway.

"Then it is settled," came a soft, clear voice from somewhere beyond Shelby's door. "We must not trouble our friend any longer, Frau McGregor. I will be more than happy to sleep downstairs."

"Who is that?" whispered Claire, inching as far into the hallway as the ornate Victorian molding would allow. "A world class skater ... and a foreign one at that ... hmmm ..."

Whitney shot Katie a stricken glance.

"You will see," the voice went on, "it is the best solution for all of us. I can begin my morning run at dawn without waking any of the other girls. And I can prepare all of my own meals. There is a good health food store in the Olympic Village, is there not?"

"Why, of *course* there is. I'll show you the way myself," crooned the housemother, obviously touched by the girl's willingness to adapt to any situation. "But I won't have you sleeping on the Halloran House couch. Not after all you've been through." She clucked loudly. "You poor little thing. A girl without a country, that's what you are. Poor, poor, little thing."

"What's the problem, Mrs. M?" asked Cyndi, slapping her towel playfully at a seething Shelby.

"As if it's any of *your* business," Shelby sniffed, with an insolent toss of her long, auburn hair.

"What concerns the skating school concerns us all, Shelby," the housemother said sharply. She turned to Cyndi. "This is Michaela Frankel, the ice dancer."

Cyndi nodded respectfully.

"Michaela defected from East Germany with her aunt, Elena Ott, leaving everyone she ever knew behind her, even her grandparents, God bless her."

Cyndi waited patiently as the housemother tsk-tsked loudly for what must have been the twentieth time.

"But that's not the worst of it," Mrs. McGregor continued. "Since skaters here aren't allowed to be housed with instructors, relatives or not, now Michaela's got nowhere to stay. And after all that turmoil!"

Cyndi threw a dirty look at Shelby, who had stationed herself in the doorway to her room like a human barricade.

"It's a wonder she didn't get on the first plane back," said Katie, coming up behind them. Claire and Whitney, unable to contain their curiosity—or maintain their awkward positions—were at her heels.

"Where are her parents?" asked Claire, extending her hand to Michaela. "Nice to meet you," she said. The East German girl smiled shyly.

"Will she be competing this year?" Cyndi asked, always willing to befriend anyone who showed enough gumption to stand up to Shelby Lang.

"Just how long does she intend to stay here?" asked Whitney, a little too bluntly.

"Only until we can find more suitable arrangements for her," answered Mrs. McGregor. "Rooms do tend to empty out in this house once in a while."

Cyndi frowned. "So what about our room? I mean, it's a little cramped, but ..."

"Yes!" gushed Claire so enthusiastically that Whitney considered smothering her with Cyndi's unused towel. "Why, she can stay with us!"

"You mean besides the fact that our suite is already overcrowded?" snapped Whitney, instantly ashamed of her Shelby-like tone of voice.

"The more the merrier," said Cyndi, smiling so broadly at Michaela that Whitney was sure her face would snap.

"But could we possibly cram another bed in there?" mused Katie aloud. Whitney cheered inwardly. Of course Katie would come to her rescue! She knew how Whitney felt about Elena Ott—and her beautiful, partner-thieving niece.

Katie paused. "Maybe we could move the dressers closer together," she suggested.

"And put in a small bed under the window," Claire added, to Whitney's consternation.

"Then it's settled," smiled the housemother, running her fingers through her white hair in obvious relief. "I'll have Mr. O'Casey bring up the rollaway from the basement just as soon as he possibly can. And since I've got a nice pot roast on for dinner, I'll just bet that he'll be on our doorstep by the stroke of six."

As the rotund woman made her way down the sweeping wooden staircase, Michaela greeted her new roommates in halting English.

"You are very kind to invite me to your room. But perhaps it would be best if I learned your names before, as you say, 'barging in'?"

"You're not barging in," insisted Claire. "And you're absolutely right—about being properly introduced. After all, we're all one big, happy family now, aren't we?"

Whitney cringed. Big, yes. Happy? No way.

"This is Katie," Claire continued, gesturing toward the tiny brunette. "She skates pairs with her twin brother, Tom."

The East German girl, clearly uncomfortable at being the center of attention, blushed to the roots of her honey-colored hair and extended her hand.

"Katie," she repeated. "You are named like our singles champion—Katarina Witt."

"That's where the similarity ends, I'm afraid," laughed Katie, who seemed pleased at the comparison anyway.

"And this is Cyndi," Claire went on, "a singles skater from the great state of Illinois."

"Cyndi," Michaela smiled. She turned her attention back to the dark-haired girl who had been doing all the introductions. "And your name?"

"Claire."

"Ah, Klara," said the young East German girl. "A very beautiful name. It comes from the Latin, I believe."

"Claire is one of the best singles skaters at the Lake Placid Skating School," Katie interrupted, beaming at her roommate proudly. "And she's not too bad off the ice, either. If you can catch her in between practices, school, and her dates with ..."

"Steeee-eeven," chanted Cyndi in her most juvenile singsong voice.

"And you?" said Michaela, turning toward Whitney, who had been trying her best to become totally invisible. "I have seen you before, yes? At the rink, with your handsome boyfriend?"

"He is *not* my boyfriend." Whitney's harsh words stung her roommates like a slap in the face, but the East German girl seemed undaunted.

"I am so sorry. Perhaps boyfriend was not the correct word to use. My English is not quite fluent yet, as you can tell."

"I think you speak English *very* well," said Katie reassuringly. "And so does Whitney, I'm sure."

Michaela smiled again. "That is your name, then, Whitney? I do not know whether there is a translation for such a truly American name."

"That's okay," Whitney replied in her sweetest voice. "It *is* a little unusual." She stood and watched as Claire took the new arrival by the arm and propelled her toward the suite, Katie and Cyndi trailing close behind them. Whitney knew that she should follow her roommates' examples and make Michaela Frankel feel welcome, but a dark feeling of foreboding held her back. Why did the East German girl *really* come to Lake Placid?

Four

"*You are* not holding the dead fish, Whitney. You are holding the partner for whom you should have affection. Now start again, please, from the beginning."

While Elena Ott rewound the taped recording of Brent and Whitney's free dance selections, the pair made their way back to the center of the ice.

"You *do* have some affection for me, don't you, Whitney?" Brent's eyes were shining with mischief. "I mean, deep, deep down somewhere."

Whitney glared into his handsome face. "Believe me, Brent, the deepest feeling I have for you at this moment is utter contempt."

"Well, that's a start, isn't it?" Chuckling, Brent swept the stray red curls off his broad forehead.

As if the two of them needed another start, thought Whitney. How many times had Elena Ott had them restart their free dance routine today? Ten? Twenty? Once for each bruise on Whitney's backside? And of the many times she had stopped them, midroutine, to point out some relatively insignificant error, how many of those flaws had been attributed to Whitney alone? That answer was easy. *All* of them.

Sneaking a sidelong glance toward the barrier, Whitney yanked her blue-and-white-pattern sweater down past her hips in anger. Why, the East German woman had her hands full just trying to rewind the tape!

Circling at an arm's length from where Brent stood adjusting the laces of his skates for what must have been the hundredth time, Whitney fumed in silence. *You must skate as though you are holding the partner for whom you should have affection, Whitney!* Elena Ott had repeated that phrase so many times in the past three days that Whitney was sure she could put it to music. Didn't the East German coach know that every time she singled Whitney out for individual correction she was undermining their team spirit? Criticizing her alone only gave Brent more reason to blame her for their every mistake. Favoritism like that would sooner or later drive Whitney's relationship with Brent even further onto the rocks.

Unless, mused a very frustrated Whitney, that was what their new coach wanted. . . .

Shocked by the thought, Whitney studied the tall, slim figure hunched over the large, portable boom box on the judges' table. Was it possible that Elena Ott was so dedicated to the idea of finding her niece a suitable partner that she would actually try to eliminate Whitney? That kind of thing only happened in a skater's nightmares, didn't it?

That was probably what Katie would say—that the anxiety generated by the Eastern competitions had finally gotten to Whitney, and she was just being paranoid.

Elena Ott clapped her hands sharply, startling Whitney back into reality.

"Places, please."

Dutifully Brent wrapped his arm around the small of Whitney's back. Whitney stretched herself into an elegant, elongated arch, draping herself over his arm.

"Now listen, Mr. Cold Hands," she murmured, smiling affectionately at her partner for her coach's benefit. "How about if you try not to drop me this time, okay?"

"You mean like this?" he whispered, letting Whitney fall at least three inches before catching her again in the grip of his strong embrace.

"You jerk!" she began, planning to give him the upbraiding of his life. But it was too late. The music had swirled into action, and with it so had they.

For this year's free dance program Brent had selected a variety of tempos and melodies from the Beatles' *Abbey Road* album. The first was a pulsing blues number danced teasingly to "Oh, Darling," followed by an upbeat rendition of "Maxwell's Silver Hammer," carefully chosen to get the pair moving and the audience clapping in time. Finally, their performance would be capped by a selection from "Something," to be skated as lovingly and longingly as possible without actually melting the ice.

But in the three days they had spent under Elena Ott's tutelage they had yet even to reach their finale. Nor were they likely to reach it today. Less than three bars into the number the couple's skates began to clash. And before they had even completed one revolution of the ice their temperaments had followed suit.

The idea behind the choreography had been simple enough. The blues number would build slowly, to showcase the couple's athleticism as well as their grace. Yet, as Whitney and Brent approached the first of their most complicated maneuvers, an inside death spiral from which Brent would pull Whitney in one smooth movement from a prone position facing the ice back onto her feet, it became clear that Brent was not paying attention.

Rather than supporting Whitney while hoisting her into an upright position, he yanked her by the arm until she felt sure that it would pop from its socket. And rather than easing her back on her feet, he hauled her in like a fisherman reeling in a fourteen-hundred pound marlin.

"And what was *that* supposed to be?" she hissed from between clenched teeth. "For crying out loud, Brent—you threw me around back there like a sack of potatoes."

Guiding his partner past the judges' table, Brent smiled as if he were performing for the crown heads of Europe and nodded perceptibly in Elena Ott's direction.

"Well, knock it off, or we'll both get kicked out of Easterns in the first round. And you aren't going anywhere without me. I'm your partner, remember?"

"Women," Brent muttered under his breath, guiding his partner into a dazzling series of dips and swirls. "You can't get anywhere with them, and you can't get anywhere without them, either."

Clasping Brent's hand in what she hoped was a painful, bone-crushing grip, Whitney pressed her small body against his in what should have been a truly romantic, cheek-to-cheek position.

"Move in closer, Whitney!" called Elena Ott, making her way out onto the ice. "Chest to chest! Hip to hip!"

Smoothly and skillfully Brent spun Whitney away from his muscular body. Then he snapped her back, like a spinning yo-yo, into a strong embrace.

Clasping her to his chest, he pulled her closer and closer until she could scarcely breathe independently of him. Almost against her will Whitney began to skate, not in time to the beat of the music, but to the relentless pounding of her heart.

"Better," Elena Ott called, nodding approvingly as Brent lifted Whitney again and again. "*Much* better."

Something in the East German coach's tone brought Whitney back to earth, causing her to be irritated and even a bit embarrassed by her demonstrative performance.

"Give me *air*," she warned in a voice as fiery-hot as the blush that had risen to her cheeks. "For heaven's sake, Brent!"

Pushing her partner away as forcefully as she could without knocking him from his skates, Whitney breathed in deeply the frigid arena air. When she finally met Brent's eyes, she could read both his pain and his anger in them.

As the tempo of their music changed, Whitney positioned herself behind her partner, waiting to catch his hand the moment he extended it between his knees. Almost instantaneously her body was snapped through his legs, yet the maneuver ended there.

Whitney went sliding the width of the arena once again, straight to the boards. Brent had not only given her all the air she wanted but a great deal of ice as well.

"*Sitzfleisch!* All the time, *sitzfleisch!*" Elena Ott jabbed at the boom box pause button with one finger. "And every landing . . ." She waved her hand in frustration as if to gather just the right words from the air. *"Mit reisenkrach!"*

Though Brent offered his hand, Whitney struggled to her feet on her own. "Maybe if she'd speak English we might actually learn something in these stupid lessons," she huffed, more loudly than she had intended.

"English? So you want it in English?" Elena Ott strode across the ice with all the single-minded determination of an invading Teutonic army. "I will be more than happy to translate my thoughts into a language you can understand."

Humiliated, Whitney busied herself with the task at hand—brushing the snow off the back of her red skating skirt. The gesture had become almost a reflex by now.

"First, *sitzfleisch*. Your uncanny ability, Miss Backman, to land on that part of your body that was designed for sitting."

Whitney could hardly believe her ears. She had just been bounced across the ice like a stone skimming across the surface of a pond! How could Elena Ott possibly blame *her* for the awkward landing?

"But *he* didn't catch me!" Whitney wailed in her own defense. "He didn't even *try*!" She glared at Brent, who looked away sheepishly.

"Nor were you in the proper position to *be* caught," snapped the coach, as tightly and definitely as a closed bear trap. "Which brings us to point number two—your landings."

Brent winked surreptitiously at Whitney from behind the wiry instructor's back.

"You land ... *mit reisenkrach*. Like a load of bricks!"

Whitney's mouth dropped open in amazement. Had she been skating alone today? Wasn't Brent at least partially responsible for what happened out on the ice?

Elena Ott rubbed her hands together briskly, as if to ward off the chill of the arena. "To correct the problem, I ask that you both spend some extra time in the ballet studio. And with the Eastern competitions only ten days away, I do not have to remind you, I think, that time is of the essence."

Whitney glanced up at the balcony overlooking the ice where the skating school's ballet studio was located. *Extra* hours! And where would they come from? Whitney shuddered. Her days were already more than full.

Elena Ott was not yet finished. "And do not think that I will not check the sign-in sheet to make sure of your attendance. I may not be so well versed in the intricacies of your native English, but the tricks of skating students?" The elderly woman smiled mysteriously. "They are the same all over the world."

"Well, I hope you're satisfied," Whitney said as their coach left the ice, bringing the lesson to an end. "It wasn't bad enough that you made me look bad at Regionals. Now Elena the Hun is blaming *me* for all of *your* mistakes!" She jabbed her toe pick violently into the ice. "You trip me with your skates, it's *my* fault. You're a butterfingers and it's my fault. It's a wonder she didn't blame me for—"

"You *weren't* in the right position you know," Brent protested. "Your arms ..."

"My arms? I'm lucky they didn't blow clean off of my body! For Pete's sake, Brent, you launched me like a torpedo!"

Her partner chuckled quietly. "I guess I did get you going a little fast. Still, that doesn't mean that I'm to blame for all of our problems."

Whitney's cheeks blazed with fury. "Why, you—"

Suddenly, from the judges' table, came a loud, implausible cough. "I am sorry to interrupt," said Elena Ott, who had returned for the boom box.

"But I should not wonder that you cannot skate to the music of love. Not when you cannot manage even to like each other."

Brent and Whitney waited in silence while the East German woman packed up her belongings and headed, once again, into the darkness of the massive arena.

"I like *you* well enough," murmured Brent under his breath, as though he suspected that Elena Ott could somehow hear them no matter how hushed their conversation.

"If you do, you have a bizarre way of showing it."

Brent shrugged his broad shoulders. "You get back what you put in, nothing more. Which is why we ended up with a new coach ten days before Easterns."

Whitney frowned. What was he talking about?

"The fact is, if you had put anything into your skating—and into your relationship with me—we wouldn't have done so badly at Regionals."

"Oh come on! Who tripped whom during the initial round? It wasn't me who turned that tango into a ... a tangle."

Brent continued as if she had not spoken at all.

"And if we hadn't done so badly at Regionals, maybe Coach Mastroni wouldn't have passed us off to a new instructor like some second-class package." Smiling, Brent gave Whitney's nose a tweak. "Why don't you give that idea some thought while *you're* working out in the ballet studio?"

"Maybe I'll do just that," Whitney called after him as he hopped off the ice and headed nonchalantly toward the locker room door. "And while I'm at it, maybe I'll give some thought to finding a replacement for *you*. And you know where I'll look first? The ASPCA!"

The words were no sooner out of her mouth than she began to regret them. What if Elena Ott really *was* trying to make it impossible for her and Brent to get along?

Making her way to the side of the rink, Whitney slipped her rubber guards over the expensive blades of her custom-fitted skates. Maybe being relegated to the ballet studio wasn't such a bad thing after all. With Katie lying in wait around every corner, newts in hand, she was certainly in no rush to go home. And with Michaela Frankel installed in their suite, there were plenty of other good reasons to avoid Halloran House.

Whitney sighed deeply. Having spent the past two hours locked in combat with the impossible Brent Marks, she would much rather exercise her body at the ballet barre than exercise her patience with Katie and her new roommate. And, for once, she would be blissfully alone.

It was nearly ten o'clock when Whitney finally breezed into the third-floor suite, feeling much better after her solitary workout.

"It is positively *freezing* in here," she exclaimed, pulling off her pink, fur-trimmed parka. "I swear I don't know how she does it, but somehow Mrs. McGregor always manages to keep this room even colder than it is outside. And I'll tell you," she continued, rubbing her arms briskly for emphasis. "It is chillier than an Eskimo's nose out there."

"I wouldn't worry much about the temperature in this room if I were you, Whitney," commented Cyndi, sprawled across her upper bunk like a worn-out robe. "I get the distinct feeling that this room is going to heat up considerably before the night is through."

"Well, I surely doubt that," crooned Whitney, suspending her dainty hands above the antique wrought-iron radiator as if to charm it into operation. "Mrs. M pinches her pennies so hard you can hear them screaming all the way up here."

"Take my word for it," offered Katie, with a forced-looking smile. "You haven't heard anything yet."

Whitney frowned momentarily, then continued getting ready for bed. "Well, I'd love to know what it is you're all getting on about," she said, pulling her heavy bedspread around her slim, shivering shoulders. "Hey, where's Michaela?"

"The question," demanded Katie, whirling in her desk chair, "is where were *you* tonight?"

"Oh, here and there," said Whitney, busily searching through the clutter on her dresser top for an emery board. "Did you miss me?"

"Did I *miss* you?" exploded Katie, leaping from the desk to the side of Whitney's bunk. "You bet I did. In fact, Tom and I *both* missed you for over an hour—sitting down in the stupid study room like a couple of compulsive nerds!"

Whitney looked from Claire to Cyndi for assistance. None was forthcoming. "Why, Katie, I ... I don't know what to say. I spent the evening at the ballet studio—just like my coach asked me to. I couldn't have known that you wanted to see me tonight. And in the study room, no less! Why, that's the last place on God's green earth I'd ..."

"Go to work on a paper? A paper that's due in less than two weeks?"

Whitney clasped one hand to her forehead as if she were Scarlett O'Hara about to perish from the heat. "Oh, no! Katie, I'm sorry. I guess it must have slipped my mind."

Katie turned away and headed toward her bunk. "That's okay," she said. "Brent couldn't bother to remember either."

Whitney looked questioningly at Claire, who only shrugged, and Cyndi, who immediately dove under the covers. Was no one going to speak to her now? She hadn't deliberately missed their study date, after all.

Long after Mrs. McGregor had rung lights out, Whitney lay awake in her bed. There was a definite change in the atmosphere of the third-floor suite. And where had Brent gone after their disastrous practice session? Had he been upset enough to forget about the meeting with Katie and Tom as well? And where had Michaela Frankel been all evening? When the East German girl had finally returned to Halloran House, she had seemed unusually quiet. Whitney sighed. She'd just have to deal with all of her headaches later—maybe tomorrow.

Five

     It almost felt as if she had been frozen under the surface of the Lake Placid ice rink.

Whitney shivered again and turned away from the icy window that separated her from any available warmth. Suddenly she sat upright in her bed. Was their window actually *open*?

Unable to believe her eyes, Whitney rubbed them violently, then looked again. Sure enough, someone had done the unthinkable and left the window open overnight.

"I can't believe it!" she stormed, whipping the blankets from her bed with such force that the green curtains were caught in a powerful counter-draft.

"And I can't believe you're even up at this hour," mumbled Claire, checking the time on the Mickey Mouse clock she kept on the floor near her lower bunk. "For crying out loud, Whitney— the little hand hasn't even reached *seven* yet...."

Sniffling loudly, Whitney slammed the window shut with a loud bang. "It's a darned good thing I did wake up," she raved, pausing long enough to release a hearty sneeze. "We'd all be frozen solid by eight o'clock."

"Okay," Whitney continued, unwilling to contain her fury a second longer. "Which one of you nature girls decided to bring the outside in?"

Katie shrugged, obviously warm as toast under her thick comforter.

"Not me," said Claire. "I was unconscious long before lights out."

"I didn't do it either," Cyndi chimed in. "The newts might have frozen to death."

Shuddering in her flannel nightgown, Whitney aimed her glare in the direction of Michaela Frankel's cot.

"I am sorry, Whitney. I am afraid that I am the culprit," the East German girl confessed, throwing off her thin cotton coverlet. "But I did it for your own good."

Whitney's mouth dropped open. What was she talking about?

Wearing only an oversized T-shirt, Michaela padded barefoot across the room as though she were immune from the chill November air. "Dry heat," she scoffed, patting the cool radiator. "It can be death to an athlete, inflaming the membranes of the nose, making it difficult to breathe...."

"What about hypothermia?" demanded Whitney. "We weren't all born three steps from Siberia, you know."

"Well, somebody sure woke up on the wrong side of the bed this morning," commented Katie.

"Don't pay any attention to her," Cyndi recommended. "She's just grumpy because the membranes in her nose are inflamed."

"Why, it must be ten degrees in here!" Whitney shouted.

"Thirty," corrected Michaela, pulling a brush through her thick, honey-colored hair. "An ideal temperature for oxygenating the blood."

"More like freezing the blood in its tracks," Whitney said.

Claire rolled out of bed and pulled a thick terry robe over her fleecy pajamas. "I don't know, Whitney," she said mildly. "Michaela may have something there. Dry heat *can* cause sinus problems. And skating with a runny nose is like skating with a broken leg."

"I do feel more alert than I usually do in the morning," added Katie, perched on the edge of her bunk like a perky parrot.

"Well, *I* feel stiffer than a frozen turkey," sputtered Whitney, infuriated by her roommates' obvious lack of sympathy. "What do you all have to say about that?"

"I say that we either compromise ..." began Claire.

"Or you can stuff it," Katie finished, with a smile that was more like a smirk.

"Well, if that's the way it's going to be, fine," Whitney replied, riffling through her drawers for the warmest clothes she owned. "But I'll tell you this," she warned, yanking a bulky fisherman's knit sweater over her uncombed mass of golden-brown hair. "Mrs. McGregor isn't going to appreciate you letting her heat escape out the window every night."

"Whitney," said Claire quietly, "I think you owe Michaela an apology, don't you?"

"No, it is *I* who owe my new friend an apology," offered the East German girl, her hazel eyes mirroring her confusion and pain. "It was thoughtless of me to subject her to my personal wishes."

Whitney ignored her and yanked a pair of fleece-lined black warm-ups over her slim hips.

"It certainly was *not*," Katie said hotly. "This is your room, too, you know. You've got a right to open the windows if you want to."

"But that doesn't mean she's got a right to pull food out of people's mouths like she did to me this morning," countered Cyndi.

"As if you really needed another Twinkie," Katie replied. "Either on your lips or on your hips."

"That's it—time out!" called Claire, obviously wanting to stop the escalating battle.

"No, *I'm* out," Whitney replied, heaving her skating bag over her shoulder. "You want the window open? *Fine.*" With one hand she threw the sash upward as far as it would go. Instantly the room was engulfed in a cyclone of chill November wind. "And just remember *this*, Katie Arden," she added from the door. "When your stupid amphibians turn into newt cubes, don't come crying to me."

Katie hardly even glanced in her roommate's direction. "And the next time your partner gets tired of picking you up off the ice," she said with a shrug, "don't *you* come whining to me."

It wasn't that Mrs. McGregor's hearty breakfasts were much of a lure for Whitney. More suitable for a campful of plaid-shirted lumberjacks than a houseful of weight-conscious teenagers, the house-mother's eat-till-you-drop, bacon-and-egg banquets were pretty weighty—especially for an ice dancer who, within the hour, would have to leap, turn, and float over the ice as if she were lighter than air.

Still, with time to spare before her early morning practice session, and needing somewhere to go, Whitney was inclined to dawdle a bit. Besides, she was still chilled to the bone, and what better place was there for her to thaw but than over a plate of steaming food?

Yet, as she entered the richly paneled Victorian dining room, she was amazed to find that, for the first morning in three months, *nothing* was steaming on Mrs. McGregor's meticulously set table. In fact, nothing even looked lukewarm—or vaguely familiar. In the center of the table, where the oversized platter heaped with scrambled eggs and crisp bacon used to go, was a large bowl filled with the kind of grain one might use to feed horses. And in place of the steaming china teapot, usually brimming with the bracing Scottish blend chosen specially by the housemother, was a tall glass pitcher filled with a mysterious, purplish-brown liquid that looked, for all practical purposes, like something the newts had left behind.

Whitney was just bending over to sniff—and possibly identify—the questionable beverage when Mrs. McGregor burst through the kitchen door.

"Well, look who's up with the rooster this morning," she said. "My favorite layabout, Whitney Backman! And not a moment too soon." The woman waggled her finger as if in warning. "There's a nip in the air today, dear."

Whitney nodded mutely.

"That's why you'd best be drinking that prune juice I warmed for you. And plenty of it, too. You wouldn't want it to get cold."

Whitney gestured cautiously toward the pitcher of thick, brown ooze. "*That's* what it is, then? Prune juice?" She shook her head in wonder. It was hard to believe that anything that disgusting had ever come from a plum. Even a dried one.

"That's exactly what it is. And if what Michaela Frankel says is true, it'll work wonders for all of you. Just swarming with vitamins, that stuff is. And warmed up a bit like it is, it won't shock your system, either."

"Oh," Whitney replied with a gulp. "Great." She pointed at the bowl of mixed grain weighing down the lace tablecloth. "And that stuff?"

"Why, it's Muesli," announced the housemother, proud to have mastered at least one word of a foreign language. "It's like granola—a mixture of oats, wheat, nuts, dates—everything that's high in fiber."

So that's what all this was about! Not only had her own roommates ganged up on her, but now Mrs. McGregor was cooking to suit Michaela Frankel! If you could call this cooking.

"This is certainly a very un-American meal," said Whitney.

"Why, of course it is," said Mrs. McGregor. "You mustn't be so critical, dearie." She wiped her hands furiously on the front of her linen apron. "You know, America is a country where anyone can come—from anywhere—and know that they'll be welcomed no matter what their language, or nationality, or ..."

"Skating title," suggested Whitney nastily.

"That's right," agreed the housemother. "And after all that poor little thing's been through." She tsk-tsked emphatically. "Why, it's the least we can do to make her feel welcome."

That was the last straw.

"What *she's* been through?" Whitney burst out. "What about what *I've* been through? First I nearly freeze to death in my own room, and now this."

The intake of Mrs. McGregor's breath was nearly strong enough to suck in everything that was on the table.

"Well, aren't we Miss High and Mighty, then!" she said finally, her hands planted firmly on her ample hips. "Three months I've toadied to your every whim, and now you're not satisfied with what I'm giving you to eat?"

Whitney winced at her own lack of tact. "I'm sorry, Mrs. M. I'm not complaining about your cooking. . . ."

The housemother crossed her arms over her chest. "You'd better *not* be. I don't see you wasting away to nothing around here."

"No, of course not. Nobody is. It's just that I'm not used to . . ."

"Sharing what you have with others who aren't quite as fortunate as you?"

Whitney groaned inwardly. She had shared her room. She had shared her friends. What was left— her skating partner?

Whitney glanced at the regulator clock centered high on the foyer wall. In less than twenty minutes she was due at the Olympic Arena for practice.

"I'm sorry, Mrs. M," she apologized again. "I've got to go." She began inching backward toward the dining room door.

"Without your breakfast? You mean you won't even try it?"

"No time, Mrs. M, really. Tomorrow I'll try it, prune juice and all. I promise."

Turning, Whitney bolted from the room.

"All right, then, Whitney, off with you. But I'm warning you," Mrs. McGregor called after her. "If *you* can't be hospitable, then we'll all have to be hospitable for you!"

Whitney sighed as she escaped down the rickety wooden steps. She had been hospitable. Why, in the past few days she had offered the East German girl everything she could, even a book to read so she could practice her English.

And what had she gotten in exchange? So far, no breakfast. And a miserable cold from the open window.

Six

Francis O'Casey, the rink caretaker, laid aside the screwdriver he was using to jimmy the lock on the office door. The elderly, New Hampshire–bred man had become as much a fixture in the Olympic Village as the Zamboni machine—the lumbering ice resurfacer he drove around the ice.

"Well, if it ain't our little hot house flowah," he greeted Whitney with a polite nod. "And lookin' every bit as rosy as the American Beauty itself."

"That's hot haouse fla-wer," Whitney responded, exaggerating her southern accent as much as she could. "Or at least that's the way we say it where I come from."

"That's what I like about you, Whitney," smiled

the caretaker, wiping his hands on the front of his coveralls. "You teach me your language, I teach you mine. That's the kind of thing that makes the world go round."

"Well, at least I know what's around the corner for today," chirped the tiny skater, inching toward the arena seats in a concerted effort to extricate herself from the talkative Zamboni operator while maintaining her southern charm. "Ice— and lots of it."

Whitney had a feeling Mr. O'Casey would keep talking all morning, and she had plenty of work to do. Where was Brent? "Well, I'd better hit the ice now," she said aloud.

Mr. O'Casey grinned. "It's good ice, too. Made it myself just this morning. Of course, the pair that was usin' it chewed it up a little."

"The pair that's been using it?" Whitney glanced up at the arena clock. Why, it wasn't even eight o'clock yet! "But Brent and I were scheduled for the first practice session. Who else was here this morning?"

The old man shrugged. "Don't rightly know."

Her curiosity piqued, Whitney hurried to the top row of the arena seats and looked down onto the massive rink. Sure enough, a couple was out on the ice.

Mr. O'Casey came to stand beside her. "Beautiful, ain't they?" He shook his head as if in disbelief. "I've seen 'em come and I've seen 'em go, but those two fit together just as natural as rubber boots on a duck hunter."

The scene that was unfolding before her almost stole Whitney's breath away. As the graceful couple made their way, weaving and twirling, around the far corner of the ice, Whitney was struck, not by their passionate elegance, but by their obvious familiarity with each other's rhythm. The girl leaped into her waiting partner's arms, twining sensually around his body like a rare flowering vine. Whitney was captivated by her spirited lightness and quietly smoldering appeal. The shy, somewhat exotic quality that Michaela Frankel had not only perfected but was now using to bewitch none other than Brent Marks!

Pressing her heavy skating bag to her chest as if to quell her thundering heartbeat, Whitney looked on in stricken amazement.

"Well, I'll be dipped, flipped, and fried," cried Francis O'Casey. "If it ain't your Brent out there! I didn't even recognize him. Why, he's catching better than a shortstop!" He nudged Whitney sharply with his elbow. "Looks like you ain't got a thing to worry about as far as Easterns are concerned. He's really improving."

"Right," Whitney murmured, moving numbly toward the ice. What could she possibly have to worry about? A partner who seemed so infuriatingly attuned with Michaela Frankel's style that even the addition of music would seem like an unnecessary distraction? A new coach who was standing there, watching as the dazzling East German champion swept Brent off his size eleven feet? The fact that her entire future was crumbling before her eyes? Why, of course, she had nothing to worry about! She had already lost everything she had to lose.

No, there *was* something she still had to lose Whitney realized, suddenly feeling disoriented on the stairs. Watching the lithe foreigner wend her way down the length of Brent's strong body for what seemed to be the hundredth time, Whitney was seized by a whirlwind of feeling so strong and so sudden it was as if everything she had ever believed—or thought she believed—had been swept away in one huge swell of emotion.

Where *had* Brent been last night? Holding tryouts for her replacement? Holding Michaela Frankel as closely as he was right now, leaving only enough distance between them for a whisper?

Suddenly Whitney could no longer contain the sob that seemed to have come straight from her heart.

"Whitney!" Elena Ott called, waving from the judges' table as if she were greeting a long-lost cousin. "You are just in time! Michaela is demonstrating a new movement that will be perfect for your waltz number!"

Whitney stood frozen as solidly on the steps as if Mr. O'Casey had Zambonied her there himself.

With a lingering, grateful glance, Brent pulled himself away from the gentle tangle of the East German girl's arms. "Hey, Whitney, get your skates on and we'll try it out."

"Try it out?" she repeated, fighting in vain to keep her voice steady.

Tossing her skate bag over her shoulder, she turned and headed blindly for the door, as confused by what she had seen as she was by her own envious tears.

Seven

"*Why can't* I just do things on my own?" Whitney said to her own reflection in the large antique wall mirror. "Why does every move I make have to revolve around him, both on the ice and off?"

Whitney closed her eyes and imagined herself back at the rink. It is all a team effort. How many times had Elena Ott said those very words in regard to the troublesome free dance routine that would take no more than five short minutes to perform, yet count for nearly half of Backman and Marks's Eastern competition score? The words had come back to haunt her in the hopelessly cluttered Halloran House suite. There was no escaping them. Or her roommates.

Clearly Katie Arden was willing to do just about anything to get Whitney to do her share of the research for their science project. She had already negotiated a tentative truce between the still-smoldering suitemates, and somehow she'd extracted a promise from Brent Marks that he would contribute his full efforts to the joint project.

Nor had Katie stopped there. To insure that Whitney would indeed show up at the next scheduled meeting, Katie was not only willing to escort her friend personally, but she offered to see to it that Whitney got there without compromising either her fashion sense or her warmth. Katie was, at that very moment, impatiently holding the shiny pink parka open for her.

"Okay, okay," Whitney said with a laugh, stuffing her arms into the fur-trimmed jacket. "But I still don't know why we've got to go to Burger Haven to do this. Really, Katie—of all the places to work on a paper about something as totally unappetizing as slimy reptiles." Pulling a comb from the pocket of her beige corduroy jeans, she gave her hair one more critical appraisal. "That kind of planning is the result of a twisted mind."

"For your information, they *aren't* reptiles," said Katie smoothly, nearly pushing her roommate through the door. "And as for Burger Haven, remember that you didn't bother to show up at all for the meeting in the study room."

"I was at the ballet studio—just like I told you," Whitney replied, thumping down the stairs with Katie right behind her.

"And of course since you chose the library as

the site for the conflict of the century, we're *all* banned from there until Hades freezes over," Katie continued.

"It shouldn't take long in this weather," Whitney complained, now shivering in the November chill.

Katie's look was decidedly unsympathetic. "So, that leaves us with Burger Haven, grease capital of the world. Hopefully it will be neutral enough territory so that the four of us can spend a couple of peaceful hours working—and share a couple of orders of fries."

Whitney walked in uncharacteristically tight-lipped silence.

"Well?" Katie demanded, her eyebrows elevated in a high, quizzical arch.

"Well what?"

"Well, we won't have to call in the National Guards to keep the peace today, will we? Because Tom and I have really about had it with the bickering between you two. If you know what I mean."

"I know what you mean," Whitney answered evenly, a note of exhaustion in her usually cheery voice. "And we won't need a referee. There won't be any fighting."

Katie wiped her forehead with one gloved hand. "Well that's a relief. And not just because of the newt thing, either. Easterns are only a week away and ..."

"Katie," Whitney began slowly, "there won't be any fighting because Brent and I aren't speaking. Or at least *I'm* not speaking to him, anyway."

"Oh, for crying out loud," moaned her roommate. "Just when you think things couldn't get any worse! What happened now? Did he drop you in slush? Did he step on your foot? What?"

"Oh, he dropped me, all right—and then he stepped on me," Whitney replied darkly, her heart overcome by the kind of dull, relentless ache that no sports doctor could remedy. Soon she found herself blurting out the entire scenario that had taken place the morning before.

Katie shook her head. "Whitney, there could be a thousand good reasons Brent was skating with Michaela."

"Just give me one," Whitney challenged.

"He was learning a new move," cried Katie, flinging her arms out straight at her sides. "Elena Ott told you so herself."

"Oh, he was learning some new *moves* all right." Whitney nuzzled the soft fur collar of her jacket with her chin. "You know as well as I do that no coach lets a pairs or dance skater take the ice with somebody who isn't his partner. It throws everything off."

"To tell you the truth, Whitney, I don't think your problem has much to do with skating."

Whitney stopped dead in her tracks. "I'm sure I don't know what you mean."

"I mean that your interest in Brent Marks goes deeper than you think. And you've waited too long to tell him so."

"But I couldn't possibly tell him the way I ... how much I ..." Suddenly Whitney's eyes were awash with bitter, remorseful tears. "Not after all that I've done."

"You mean there's *more*?" Katie rolled her eyes heavenward.

Trudging along minutes later, Whitney poured out the story of her first—and last—disastrous date with Brent. She had never told anyone about it, and now it felt good to get the whole thing off her chest.

"It wasn't a date, really," she explained. "It was a celebration, just after the summer preview competitions. The two of us went to dinner at a quaint little inn. It was no big deal, really."

"Was there a candle on the table?" Katie demanded.

"Well, yes, I suppose there was."

"Then it was a *date*—pure and simple."

Whitney shook her head violently. "No way. Our coach back in Atlanta wouldn't allow us to date. 'Kiss your partner and you'll kiss the boards.' That's what she always said, anyway." She pulled her collar more tightly to her chin. "To Brent, the dinner was more than just a celebration, though."

"You mean, he told you the way he felt about you," persisted Katie.

"He told me that he wanted to be more than partners." Whitney smiled ruefully. "He even kissed me."

"He *kissed* you?" shrieked Katie, drawing the attention of nearly everyone on Lake Placid's main street. "What was it like?"

Whitney's grin was wistful. "It felt warm ... and sort of swirly ... and *right*. And that's why I had no choice but to do what I did."

Katie gasped. "You didn't ..."

"Yep. I slapped him."

"Oh, no!" Katie groaned.

Whitney shrugged helplessly. "It was only a little slap, really."

"Well, a little slapping can go a long way," frowned Katie. "But you've probably realized that by now."

"The proof is right there in black and white, every time we get our competition scores. I haven't even wanted Brent to touch me when we're skating. If we get too close . . ."

Katie finished her sentence. "You'll kiss the boards."

"Exactly." Whitney daubed at her turned-up nose with a bedraggled tissue. "Well, whenever Brent feels me pull away, he gets angry."

"And then you lapse into your specialty—the Backman Butt Slide."

Whitney nodded miserably. "So now what do I do?"

Katie guided her friend into the crosswalk opposite the Burger Haven. "You'll have to tell him just how you feel—soon, before things get worse. And certainly before Easterns."

"But what about Michaela? If you could have seen . . ."

"Uh-uh," warned Katie, holding one finger aloft as if to silence a petulant child. "The Michaela bit is all in your mind. I'm sure of it."

Pulling the crumpled tissue out of her roommate's hand, Katie wiped the tears away from Whitney's face. "Tell him the truth. Then you won't have anything more to worry about." Katie grinned momentarily, then continued in her most authoritarian voice. "Except this paper. Which, by the way, is due ..."

Whitney sighed. "In less than a week. I know, I know."

Topped with a blinking neon burger, the Burger Haven was surrounded on three sides with windows and was hardly private.

Tom Arden was pressing his face firmly against the window near the booth as the two of them approached.

"That's my twin," beamed Katie, stopping long enough to thumb her nose at her brother before hurrying toward the automatic doors. "But you probably noticed the family resemblance."

Hearing no response, she turned back to Whitney standing stock-still in her Reeboks.

"Hey, Ice Princess!" Katie called, her hands jammed firmly in the deep pockets of her down jacket. "It's cold out here. Don't tell me you haven't noticed."

Still Whitney did not reply.

"Whitney! *Hey*," Katie repeated, jogging back to her roommate's side. "I can guarantee you— whatever it is you're looking at, it'll look even better from inside."

Whitney pointed to the window in horror.

There, in a booth less than three steps away from Tom, sat Brent and Michaela with a single milk shake between them.

"I'm out of here," said Whitney, spinning so

abruptly on the heel of her sneaker that it was a wonder she didn't burn rubber.

"But you *can't* . . . Oh, Whitney," moaned Katie, left alone again with her books and her brother.

Sprinting blindly past the rows of quaint shops and charming cafés, her gold-brown hair blowing behind her like a billowing sail, Whitney couldn't stop to feel guilty about leaving Katie and Tom to their studies. If Brent Marks had busied himself with his own "research" then she had made some important findings of her own.

And although her methods might have been a little less than scientific, Whitney had gathered all the objective evidence she needed, more than any research volume—or her breaking heart—could possibly hold.

Eight

He had called her selfish. Spoiled. A pampered and petted southern prima donna whose attention span was limited to two areas of interest: what her next indulgence would be, and how soon that indulgence was likely to arrive.

But it was not an interest in herself that brought Whitney to the Olympic Arena five days before the Eastern Championships. Nor was it her own disappointment and hurt that was about to bring her face to face with the stern, uncompromising man most of the skaters took care to avoid, just as carefully as they skirted the bumps and gouges that marred the surface of the rink.

Gulping back her pride as well as her fear, Whitney hesitated at the steel door that separated the small corner office from the rest of the huge arena. There were ten minutes to spare before Gregory Mastroni was scheduled for his next lesson—still plenty of time for Whitney to run through the speech she had prepared one last time.

Bundling her hands in the folds of her oversize Scandinavian sweater, she paced before the door, silent as a cat in her leather sneakers, repeating the flat, unyielding statements she knew Brent wanted to say, yet never would.

"Practice makes perfect," rang a familiar voice in Whitney's ear, causing her to jump. "Or at least, that's what they say. As I see it, sometimes practice just makes *average*. And other times it makes a mess. All depends on what you're practicin'."

Mr. O'Casey lifted the ear flaps of his plaid hunting camp. "That *is* what you're here for, ain't it? Practice?"

"Uh, kind of," Whitney replied, a bit embarrassed. Had the caretaker heard her talking to herself?

"You're wanting to see Coach Mastroni, then," said Mr. O'Casey helpfully. "Well, all you've got to do is knock." He smiled, extending one jacketed arm dangerously near the steel door.

Whitney held her breath.

Sensing her reluctance, the wizened old man bent closer and whispered conspiratorially, "Seems like knockin' on a grizzly's den, I know. But strictness, well, that's just Coach Mastroni's way. He ain't one for showin' his feelings—or at least, not his softer feelings, if you know what I mean."

Whitney nodded numbly. Having spent her first three months on Lake Placid hiding her own real feelings for Brent, she had learned firsthand how keeping one's emotions inside could make one as testy as a bear.

"Still, if a body's got somethin' to say, it's best to say it and be done with it," Mr. O'Casey said gently.

"Okay," answered Whitney weakly, by now so bewildered by the meandering path of the work-man's conversation that she had almost lost track of her reason for being there at all.

"That's just what I thought you'd say," he smiled, leaning over to pound three times loudly on the heavy steel door. "Coach, there's somebody waitin' to see you out here. And she ain't gettin' any younger standin' out in the hall."

"Send her in then." The voice seemed as taut as a live wire—and even more dangerous.

"See? That's all there is to it," Francis O'Casey announced. He ushered the girl inside and closed the door behind her.

Devoid of decoration, containing only a few neatly arranged shelves, a large pine desk, and a black, utilitarian telephone, the room seemed every bit as austere and to the point as the man who occupied it. Whitney cleared her throat.

"Look, Whitney," said Coach Mastroni, running his hand carefully through his short brown hair, "if you're here to talk to me about Elena Ott, I'm afraid there's nothing I can do. I know she's tough, but she's the best ..."

"I'm not," blurted Whitney. "I mean, she's not

the problem." Whitney reconsidered the accuracy of her words, then began again. "I mean, she's not the *only* problem. . . ."

Gregory Mastroni pushed himself away from the desk. "I've been watching you skate since September, Whitney. I think I know what the problem is. . . ."

"I want a new partner," said Whitney, nearly knocked back in shock at the force of her own words. What had happened to the flowery speech she had prepared? And what was it about the intensity of Gregory Mastroni's piercing brown eyes that seemed to evaporate all of her confidence?

The former Olympic champion didn't even blink. "Well, if *that's* all it is," he replied as though she had burst in to report nothing more pressing than a rise in the temperature, "why didn't you say something sooner?"

Whitney felt as though a tremendous weight had been hoisted from her shoulders. "You mean, it's not a big deal?"

Coach Mastroni tapped his pencil thoughtfully against the thin line of his lips. "No big deal at all. Not to me, anyway."

Whitney could hardly believe her luck. Had she just managed to catch him in a rare good mood?

"Well, you have no idea how happy I am to hear you say that, Coach Mastroni," she said. "I mean, you know that Brent and I get along like two wet cats in the same burlap bag. And it's obviously been affecting our skating. I guess I shouldn't be surprised that your answer is . . ."

"My answer is *no*, Whitney."

While Whitney reeled in confusion, the lanky ex-skater leaned across his desk as if preparing to pounce. "How dare you ask me to release you from your partnership less than a week before Easterns? What do you think this is, a debutante ball? Some kind of fancy adolescent cotillion where you can just cross someone off your dance card and waltz away?"

"Well, n-no," she stammered, her mind awhirl with the sudden turn of events.

"Then how could you be so unprofessional? So ... *irresponsible*?" Coach Mastroni slapped his pencil against the desktop in frustration. "Not that I'm surprised to hear that your partner means nothing to you. That certainly shows in your skating. In fact, the only thing that surprises me is that it wasn't Brent who came in here asking for a replacement. A replacement for *you*, Whitney."

Whitney felt herself coloring to the roots of her honey-blond hair.

"But do you know what really shocks me about this whole matter, Whitney?" Gregory Mastroni wheeled in his seat abruptly.

Whitney knew better than to answer.

"The fact that this school doesn't mean anything to you. That you would single-handedly ruin our chances for a gold medal in Rhode Island just to prove some ridiculous point. That you would take yourself out of contention less than one week before Easterns rather than skate with a partner you don't like."

"Well, we're not exactly Torvill and Dean, are

we?" she replied hotly, surprised by her defensive retort as was the skating school director. "We barely made it past Regionals. . . ."

"And you may very well just scrape by at Easterns, but the fact is that you're the best we've got." The skating school director stared at the neatly printed roster that hung on the bulletin board behind him. "For the time being, anyway."

Whitney arched an eyebrow. What was *that* supposed to mean? That the coach would make do with Whitney and Brent until the younger ice dance couples had been properly prepared for the rigors of competition? Or only until Michaela Frankel was ready to launch herself into the fray with the Lake Placid banner in one hand and Brent in the other?

Whitney looked up to find Gregory Mastroni lost in contemplation, his eyes scouring every detail of her anxious, unhappy face.

"Still, I suppose you can't skate your best with a partner you can't even manage to like, can you?" he said finally.

"I guess not," answered Whitney unhappily. It had taken her nearly six years to realize how much she *did* like Brent. How long would it take her to stop caring for him? The thought was enough to make her shudder.

"I'll tell you what," offered the coach, turning away from her. "You stay with Brent through Easterns—"

"But I can't. . . ."

He silenced her with a wave of his hand.

"If you don't place at Easterns, I promise you I'll consider your request."

"Oh! Th-thank you!" she stammered, inching toward the door before the irascible coach had time to change his mind. "Thank you. Really."

"But Whitney," he called after her, his voice suddenly heavy with concern.

The girl popped her head back through the door.

"The thing is—sometimes you don't really know what you've got until it's gone. Do you know what I'm getting at?"

Whitney blanched. A week ago those words would have meant nothing to her, yet now they seared into the deepest recesses of her heart.

"I think so," she replied.

"Then just give it a little thought when you get a chance. Okay?"

Whitney nodded, her eyes brimming with tears. "Okay."

Nine

The music blaring at top volume from the small, German-made clock radio under Michaela's rollaway bed was enough to jolt all four girls out of their dreams—and nearly sent a still-snoring Cyndi rolling off the edge of her upper bunk.

"Okay, I get the message," groaned Katie, yanking the blanket over her head. "It's morning."

"And what do you know," mumbled Claire sleepily. "It came at exactly the same time today as it did yesterday."

"That still doesn't explain what in the world's so good about it," said Cyndi, clinging to the edge of her perch.

"What is so *gooot* about it?" sang Michaela,

springing about the cluttered room as if it had been designated the finish line for her predawn run. "Why, it is a new and beautiful day!"

Yanking back the dusty green curtains as if she were unveiling an artistic masterpiece, she stood in rapt amazement at the sparkling wonderland outside the third-floor window.

"Such a room," she gasped, in sincere wonderment. "And such a view! Why, from this room you can see the lake, the mountains ..."

"And the gas station on the corner," laughed Katie.

"And the Burger Haven sign," added Cyndi with a sigh.

"I'll tell you what we can see in this room," sputtered Whitney, nearly mummified by the four woolen blankets she had wrapped around her tiny body for the night. "Our breath!" Struggling upright, she panted once into the frosty air, which condensed into a wispy, short-lived cloud.

"But I opened the window only halfway," offered Michaela, by way of apology. "Just as we agreed."

"That must be why I'm only half-frozen," Whitney said.

As usual, Claire was the first to brave the chill and throw off the covers that insulated her from the especially well-ventilated room.

"Oh, come on, Whitney, it's really not so bad," she said, padding across the room as casually as if she were strolling a warm Bermuda beach.

Whitney leaped suddenly out of her upper bunk, bedclothes and all, and yanked a striped towel off the wall-mounted rack. Seconds later she was unlocking the door to the hallway, still dragging the tangled quilts behind her.

"Where are you going?" Cyndi asked in surprise.

"To the only warm spot on this floor. The shower."

"Like *that*?"

"Certainly," Whitney replied, pulling her soap and toothpaste into the folds of her bedding. She couldn't wait to take a nice hot shower.

Two minutes after reaching the bathroom, Whitney was back in the suite.

"There's no hot water," she gasped, standing in a sodden puddle on the worn, wall-to-wall carpet. "It's ten degrees in this room and *there's no hot water!*"

"You are welcome," replied Michaela cheerfully, passing her roommate a dry towel.

From behind the door Claire gestured wildly at Michaela, but to no avail.

"Hot water is very bad for the blood vessels," the East German girl went on, still extending the towel. "Very bad for the whole circulatory system. That is why I make sure that it is lukewarm only."

Grabbing a handful of her dripping hair, Whitney rung it out like a sponge onto the now-squishy rug.

"Are you telling me that *you* had something to do with the fact that there is no hot water?" Whitney tried hard to keep the tone of her voice even.

The tawny-haired girl blinked. "You are welcome," she repeated.

"I don't believe this!" Whitney said to no one in particular. "Not *here*. Not in *my* room."

"Oh, come on, Whitney," coaxed Claire. "She didn't mean any harm."

"Harm? Claire, in three days I leave for Rhode Island where I get to compete in Easterns with a head cold that just won't quit." And a partner who can't wait to quit, she added to herself, tossing the towels to the floor in a soggy heap.

As Whitney rummaged wildly through her closet for the warmest clothes she could find, Michaela sank onto the mattress of the rollaway bed and buried her face in her hands. "I only wanted to help," she said.

"And you wanted to get your claws into my skating partner, too," Whitney retorted. The words were out before she could stop herself.

So sharp was Whitney's intake of breath in the small, cluttered suite that the windows seemed to rattle in their frames.

"Whitney!"

"I mean it, Katie—either *she* goes, or I go." Whitney wrenched a black woolen turtleneck over her still-dripping hair. "Which of us is it going to be?"

Whitney watched as a glance was passed from Claire to Katie to Cyndi.

"Fine," Whitney replied, tossing her toilet items into her already overburdened skate bag. "If that's the way you want it, then fine. You can all freeze to death in here as far as I'm concerned."

"Where are you going?" asked Cyndi, sounding worried.

"First, I'm going to the locker room to get some hot water," Whitney answered, throwing her pink parka over her shoulders like a cape.

"And after I steam and scald and scour myself until every blood vessel in my body bursts, *then* I'm going to practice. That is, if I still have a partner," she added to herself as she closed the door behind her.

Ten

     "Again," called Elena Ott, tucking the stray strands of her upswept, yellow-gray hair behind her ears. "Let's take it from the reprieve."

"A reprieve," scoffed Whitney as they headed back over the ice. "Isn't that what they give people in prison?"

"Not in *this* prison." Brent dusted the frosty remnants of his partner's last fall from the back of her green skating skirt. "We're lifers."

That's what you think, thought Whitney, anchoring herself into position with a violent jab of her scuffed white skate. What would Brent do when he discovered that she had been to see the only person who could commute their sentence? How would he react to the news that he was finally being set free? That he would finally get the chance to practice his new moves with the only ice dancer who would be able to take his errors in stride: Michaela Frankel herself?

After counting down the lingering beats that led into the reprieve, Whitney and Brent launched into action, wrapped loosely around each other like a pair of discarded gloves. Coach Mastroni had said he would wait until after Easterns to make his decision. He wanted to be sure that there was no improvement in the situation before making his decision. But now, moving across the ice like an automaton, Whitney was certain that no improvement was possible. For despite the haunting beauty of the music, she and Brent skated to "Something" as if it were *nothing*. They were only going through the motions of the choreography.

Yet, as the music reached a crescendo, Whitney couldn't help but succumb to the intensity of the moment—and the strong hand at her hip. In one graceful move she propelled herself up and over Brent's back. But as she coiled her body around his, waiting for the strong grip that would guide her, the grip did not come. Seconds later she was being dragged across the rink like a small scrap of paper that had stuck to the bottom of her partner's skate.

"It is not working," announced Elena Ott. She had become so accustomed to the portable boom box by now that she could jab the stop button without even looking. "It is not working at *all*."

"My partner isn't working," complained Whitney, hauling her battered body once again off the burning-cold ice.

"But you misunderstand me." The elderly East German tapped her chin thoughtfully with the tip of her index finger. "It is not the twist itself that has gone wrong, but the decision."

"What decision?" murmured Brent, taking Whitney's elbow in his hand, only to have her shake it free of his grasp.

"Maybe she means the decision to have Michaela meet you here after practice," Whitney snapped, nodding in the direction of the arena seats. "Look at that—only three rows back. Your own little audience."

Noticing for the first time the arrival of the tawny-haired girl who sat half-hidden in the shadows of the massive building, Brent waved casually in her direction. "She must be here to see her aunt," he explained, straightening the hem of his bulky tweed sweater. "I never asked her to ..."

"Silence!" Elena Ott banged on the judges' table for emphasis. "For two people who cannot seem to bear even to speak to one another, you certainly need a great deal of discussion."

"What is she talking about?" Brent turned to his partner in obvious confusion. When Whitney would not meet his questioning eyes, he put an arm around her waist and pulled her closer to their waiting coach.

"At first I thought—as did Mr. Mastroni—that the decision itself might put a little ..." The foreigner waved one hand in the air. "*Distanz* between you. That just thinking of finding new partners might somehow bring you closer together."

"New partners?" Brent wheeled on his skates

until he was eye-to-eye with Elena Ott. "Who's finding a new partner?"

The elderly woman arched one gray brow in surprise. "According to Coach Mastroni, you are. Of course."

"I am?" Brent began to chuckle, then laugh, as if to prove that this were nothing more than a joke. "No, Coach Ott," he said finally, "I'm afraid you're mistaken. I never said anything to Coach Mastroni about a new partner!"

Whitney paled.

Brent turned toward her. "You don't think this is funny, do you? Do you know something about this?"

Grabbing her by the shoulders, he shook her like a rag doll. "You actually went to Coach Mastroni *behind my back* and asked him ..."

"For a new partner," snapped Elena Ott. "As you had decided. And unless you manage to place in the upcoming Eastern competitions, you will get your wish."

"You bet," Brent said angrily, his eyes burning like two glowing lumps of coal. As if seared by their intensity, Whitney stared down at the ice.

How dare he give her those big, brooding eyes! He didn't want to skate with her! It would only have been a matter of time until he approached Coach Mastroni himself.

Whitney glared as Brent yanked his fingers furiously through his curly red hair. It was just his ego. First she had spurned his romantic advances, and then she had delivered the coup de grace— dumping him before he'd had a chance to dump her! Whitney folded her arms across her chest. Right now he was probably concerned about how he appeared to her replacement, who was watching the action intently from the arena seats. No doubt she was wondering if she would fit into Whitney's costumes as neatly as she had squeezed into Brent's arms. The arms that were holding her now more tightly than they had ever held her before.

"It isn't right, Whitney," he whispered, his voice full of emotion. "After six years! I don't know if I could . . ."

"You don't know if you could *what*?" she shot back, avoiding his eyes. "Wait a few more days to get rid of me? Hold out until after Easterns to trade in one slightly used American partner for a new German model?"

He released her in disgust. "I don't know why we should bother competing in Easterns at all."

Whitney stared at Brent in shock. So he had been out to dump her before she dumped him! If he wasn't the most conceited, self-centered . . .

"*Dummkopf!*" cried Elena Ott, summing up Whitney's feelings even more emphatically than she could have herself. "How do you expect to attract the right kind of partner *unless* you perform in Rhode Island?"

Brent leaned sullenly against the rails. "You've got a point there, Coach Ott," he sighed. "I guess that means we're stuck with each other."

"For the time being," Whitney said.

"Then, for the time being, you must practice," the coach interrupted, "until your free dance is perfected."

"But we can't practice now," Whitney pointed out. "I've got a class to go to. And *Brent* ..." She jerked her head in Michaela's direction. "Well, he'll find *something* to keep him busy."

Elena Ott stuffed the huge boom box into a large canvas bag. "Then you will have to practice tonight," she said. "Off the ice."

Whitney swallowed hard. Not the ballet studio again? And being shut into the tiny balcony with Brent Marks would only add fuel to the fire.

"I will let them know to expect you in the ballet studio no later than seven o'clock this evening. That gives you plenty of time to digest your studies and your dinner. Good-bye now." Slinging the canvas bag over her shoulder, the instructor turned away.

"But Coach Ott," Whitney pleaded, her voice as soft and clingy as Spanish moss. "I'm sure you'll see more improvement tomorrow if we can just spend a little time away from each other...."

"Seven o'clock—both of you. And don't forget—I will be checking the sign-in sheet tomorrow."

Whitney was sure she heard the East German woman chuckle as she headed to join her patiently waiting niece.

Eleven

It was precisely six thirty-five when Whitney climbed the spiral staircase that led to the ballet studio.

Entering the small empty room, she popped an old videotape into the machine in the corner and dropped heavily into a chair. She had chosen the tape from the skating school video library in a fit of restlessness. It had been a hard day.

Although she had specifically requested a tape so old that it had been converted to videotape from black-and-white film, Whitney knew as the picture filled the screen that she was watching more than just the image of a long-past championship performance. There was something about this ice dance couple that made Whitney shift uncomfortably in her oversize, electric-blue sweatshirt.

Fiddling nervously with the cutoff neckline of her soft, fleece-lined sweatshirt, Whitney watched as the couple whirled gracefully and naturally in each other's arms, leaving nothing but a languid memory of each elegant movement in their wake.

Still, there could be no question about it—it had been more than affection that had qualified Jim Sladky and Judy Schwomeyer for the 1972 world ice dance competitions. Brent Marks let his partner down like some sliding, shifting overload to be dumped unceremoniously off the end of a trunk, but Jim Sladky set his partner down delicately upon each note of the music. And if Whitney occasionally hit the ice with all the force of an invading army, then Judy touched down gently, as if she were supported by a warm, uplifting breeze rather than by her partner.

But what was of even more interest to Whitney was the fact that this pair had broken her former coach's cardinal rule. During the four-and-a-half minutes in which they had flawlessly performed their romantic free dance routine, they had revealed not only their love for the sport but their love for each other. And in the end they had won more than a bronze medal in the world championships—they had won each other's heart. Jim Sladky and Judy Schwomeyer were married shortly afterward.

Suddenly Whitney sat upright and switched off the sound on the studio VCR. Then she slumped back in her chair again and chewed her nails thoughtfully. What if their coach back in Atlanta had been wrong? Maybe kissing your partner had nothing at all to do with kissing the boards. And what if, by teaching Whitney to trust in her partner and not her own feelings, the well-meaning coach had unknowingly cheated her pupil out of her chance to be a partner both on and *off* the ice?

"What if we added that little extra kick to our program?" said Brent, coming up behind her and tossing his jacket into the corner of the small mirrored studio.

Whitney started but recovered quickly. "Well, you'd probably either drop me, let go of me, or throw me, same as always," Almost instantly she regretted the sharpness of her words.

"It's true," Brent admitted, pulling off his black high-top sneakers. "I haven't been the best partner lately, I know."

Whitney stared at the slatted wooden floor, speechless. Was he actually *apologizing*?

"Still, when it comes to really dropping somebody, it's you who are the pro, Whitney." Sweeping a stray red curl away from his forehead, Brent leaned casually against the ballet barre that traversed the small studio. "There's a big difference between letting go of somebody on the ice and icing them out completely." Brent shrugged his broad muscular shoulders. "Okay—so I have a tendency to drop you now and then, but—"

"Now and then?" Whitney gestured toward the ugly bruises that showed through her white ballet tights like faint grape juice stains. "Why, you bounce me around like an old tire!"

"The point is, Whitney," scowled Brent, "if I drop you, you get back up again. If you drop me, I stay dropped. Permanently." He shook his head. "After six years of . . ."

"Hard work and frustration, we're still not getting our act together on the ice," Whitney finished. "Not like we ought to be two days before Easterns. Not like *that*."

Whitney gestured toward the VCR, regretting her offhand comparison as soon as she had made it. For there, on the flickering screen, Judy Schwomeyer was all but melting into her partner's waiting arms.

"Well, not like *that*, exactly," Whitney murmured, stumbling over her words. "I mean, together."

Brent's laughter filled the room as if reflected by the floor-to-ceiling mirrors in the studio.

"I mean, they're romantic," Whitney went on, shaking her head as if to erase her own words even as she spoke them. "But they're romantic in a technically precise sort of way."

"You mean, like this," replied Brent, nestling his arm into the curve of her waist and sweeping her completely off her sneakered feet, his eyes gazing deeply into hers.

"Y-yes," she stammered, her knees suddenly weak and wobbly. Pausing long enough against the barre to catch her breath as well as her runaway emotions, she corrected herself again. "I mean *no*. You can't compare us to that couple, Brent. What they've perfected . . ."

"Is romance—both on the ice and off," Brent finished for her. "And we haven't had much of a chance to practice that ourselves, have we?" he added with a mischievous grin.

Whitney felt the color rise to her cheeks. What did Brent think—that love was something you practiced like a complicated lift until you finally got it right? Turning her back on her partner, she switched off the VCR and yanked the tape out in anger.

"Can't we at least give it a try?" Brent pleaded. "I mean, we *are* here to practice what we're not so good at, aren't we?" He took the tape gently from her hand and stuck it into the folds of his jacket. "With only two days before Easterns, we should be doing something other than arguing. We've already got *that* down to a science."

Whitney couldn't help chuckling. "I guess we have logged in more hours cutting each other down then we have at perfecting lifts, haven't we?" She knotted her voluminous sweatshirt deftly at her hip. "So where do you want to start?"

"How about beginning with what seems to be giving us the most trouble?" Brent suggested, giving his thighs a quick stretch at the barre. "How about the Frankel Twist?"

It was as if he had waved a red flag at an angry bull. Before Brent knew what was happening, Whitney was at him.

"Hey!" Brent protested, holding her at arm's length. "Take it easy!" He let go and she collapsed onto the large red throw pillows on the floor.

"Look," he went on," I know we haven't exactly been close lately. . . ."

Close enough to order each other around—but not close enough to order one shake with two straws, thought Whitney, remembering the cozy scene she had witnessed through the Burger Haven windows.

"But I can't understand why, after six years, you couldn't just tell me if you were unhappy." Brent reached out gingerly for her hand. "You know how I feel about you. You're a lot more to me than only a partner, even if you don't want to be. But to request a change behind my back ..."

"Behind your back?" snapped Whitney, shaking her hand free of his grip. "Why, while I was stuttering and stammering in Mastroni's office, you were already holding auditions for a new partner. What did you expect me to do—wait for an announcement in *Skating* magazine? To throw you a party complete with chocolate milk shakes and two straws?"

"Milk shakes?" Brent laid one hand on his partner's furrowed forehead. "I don't know about you, Whitney. With all that bouncing around you've been doing tonight, I think something might have finally shaken loose."

"That's probably what you had in mind, too," Whitney retorted, luching to her feet to meet her partner eye-to-eye. "To shake me loose so that you could skate off into the Berlin sunset with Michaela Frankel."

"The Berlin sunset?" Brent regarded his partner with undisguised amusement.

Whitney sniffed. "Well, at least as far as Nationals. She is an established champion, after all."

Without a word Brent retrieved the videotape from his jacket and inserted it back into the VCR. Instantly the screen sprang to life.

"Do you suppose Jim and Judy Sladky ever had

any bad times to go through?" Brent asked, his eyes riveted to the screen.

"Well, of course," Whitney replied, a little irritated by her partner's obvious question. "Everybody has them now and then."

"And do you think it ever occurred to Jim Sladky to replace *his* partner—because of a bunch of stupid arguments?" Brent persisted, his breath soft and even on Whitney's neck.

"I suppose not," she answered, flustered by Brent's closeness and the furious pounding of her heart.

"That's right, Whitney. He wouldn't leave his partner, no matter what. Because he loved her."

Whitney swallowed hard.

"Come on, Whitney," Brent whispered, his voice low and husky in her ear. "Tell Mastroni you've changed your mind."

"But I *haven't*," she answered, steeling herself against the tempest of emotions swirling in her heart.

He pulled her to him, cupping the tip of her delicate chin in the palm of his hand. "Then let me change it for you."

But as he drew her even closer, lowering his handsome, chiseled face to meet hers, he was met not by her petal-soft lips, but by a resounding slap so loud that it continued to echo through the small studio long after the sting had died away.

"I can't believe you!" Brent shouted, clapping his hand to his face as if to cover the lingering red imprint to her anger.

"And I can't believe just how far you'll go to make sure you get to compete at Easterns," Whitney cried, yanking the tape from the machine with such force that it flew, Frisbee-style, halfway across the room. "Oh, I know what you're thinking, Brent Marks. 'Be nice to Whitney and she'll be nice to you. Give her a kiss and maybe she'll help you get some nice high scores for artistic merit. Then, after the competition's over, you can dump her like a load of cement.' "

Dragging Whitney toward him by the hem of her blue sweatshirt, Brent knocked her forehead gently. "What is this made of—wood? Why can't you get it through your thick skull that I *care* about you! I'm not going to dump you, for Pete's sake!"

Folding his arms around her like strong, protective wings, he pinioned her to the wall facing him. "Whitney, give me a break—I'm not going anywhere! Can't you see that?"

Tearing herself out of his grip, Whitney stomped to the corner, picked up the orange satin baseball jacket, and hurled it into her partner's arms.

"Oh, you're going somewhere, Brent Marks," she declared, her voice as sharp and even as a razor blade. "Out of this studio and out of my life!"

"You want me gone?" he replied, straightening his shoulders. "Then fine, I'll go." He stepped toward his partner and met her glare head-on. "With no regrets. But I can't regret kissing you, Whitney." He shrugged into his jacket.

"Good-bye, Brent."

"Yeah, okay." He leaned in the doorway. "Just remember this, Whitney—no matter what happens, I'll always think of *you* as my partner."

Listening to his footsteps echo on the cold steel of the spiral staircase, Whitney sank to the floor and pressed her fingers to her lips, as if to capture the memory of his kiss there forever. Then she drew herself together. She was going to forget about Brent Marks as best she could.

But she couldn't push aside her doubts. What if she really was wrong about Brent's interest in Michaela Frankel?

Pulling the fur-trimmed parka over her sweats, she tossed and turned the videotape in her hand. She wasn't going to be able to sleep tonight, she knew—and not because of an open bedroom window, either.

Twelve

Glancing furtively toward the swinging kitchen door, Whitney pulled off her shoes and crept in her stocking feet across the polished hardwood floor. There was no need to announce her arrival—at least, not until she had accomplished her mission. For it wasn't every day that Whitney Backman turned over her weapons to the enemy. For she had finally decided to overcome her own stubbornness and apologize—first to her partner, and then to her East German roommate.

"Well, well—look who's come back to the plantation!" cried Mrs. McGregor, emerging from the kitchen.

"I'm not late, am I, Mrs. M? There's still an hour before curfew."

"There may be an hour before you're due, but as far as dinner's concerned, you're not a minute too soon. Do you realize I've been holdin' your plate for you since seven o'clock?"

"I didn't mean for you to wait dinner for me, Mrs. McGregor," she said, willing her empty stomach not to growl until she was safely out of the housemother's earshot. "And I don't think I really have time to ..."

The housekeeper yanked a single, ornately carved dining room chair away from the antique table. Whitney fell into it obediently.

"That's the trouble with you girls," warned the woman, waggling her fleshy finger. "Arguments, boys, those you have got time for. But a good, nutritious meal? It's strictly eat and run in this house."

Or at least it had been, Whitney thought, until Mrs. McGregor had replaced her famous pot roast with soyburger casserole and hot mashed barley.

"What *is* for dinner anyway, Mrs. M?" Whitney called into the industrial-sized kitchen.

"See for yourself," answered the housemother, manuevering her bulk through the swinging kitchen doors and setting a steaming plate on the table. Skeptically Whitney began to examine the offering with the tines of her fork.

"This *looks* like chicken pot pie," she said, spearing a piece of meat and holding it up to the light of the converted gaslamp that hung over the mahogany table.

"Of course that's what it looks like! That's what it is!" The elderly woman stepped back as if to admire her own culinary artistry. Whitney spooned up a dollop of rich brown sauce and sniffed.

"And?"

"My own sour cream gravy. Nothing less."

Whitney put down her utensils in surprise. "But I was expecting ... I don't mean to insult you, Mrs. McGregor, but this isn't exactly health food."

The round housemother planted her hands firmly on her ample hips. "Well, you've been eatin' it for three months now and you *seem* healthy enough. At least, healthy enough to run roughshod over an old woman's feelings."

"But what about Michaela?" Whitney said, beginning to feel ravenous again.

Mrs. McGregor shrugged. "The fact is, she's movin' out."

Whitney pushed herself away from the table, plate in hand, and bolted to the dining room door.

"*Now* where are you going off to?" the housemother demanded. "And with my good china, to boot?"

"Michaela!" Whitney called back, her mind already racing up the three flights of stairs between the foyer and her room. "There's something I have to say to her before she goes."

"And what might that be?"

Whitney paused for a moment. "What else?" she answered cheerfully. "I'm going to say goodbye!"

Bounding down the third-floor hall, Whitney entered the suite to find even more chaos than

she'd expected. Not only was Michaela Frankel
busily filling her suitcases with pristine stacks of
crisply ironed clothes, but Katie was busy, too,
cramming more skating gear than Whitney had
ever seen into a bag at least two sizes too small.

"Okay, who ordered the pot pie?" said Whitney,
extending the plate toward Claire.

"Just toss it into Katie's suitcase," suggested
Claire, winking at Whitney in amusement. "She
says she's going to sort it all out later."

"Never mind, Claire," said Katie, throwing her
weight across the luggage in an effort to get the
suitcase locked—or at least, closed. "I'm not about
to turn up short of stuff in Rhode Island."

"Suit yourself," Claire replied with a shrug.

"Oh, for crying out loud," panted Katie, jump-
ing back from the suitcase just in time for the
overstuffed bag to let loose an avalanche of
rolled-up tights, bulky sweaters, and wrinkled skirts.
"You know what I mean. At the summer previews
I ripped *three* pairs of tights. Did I think to bring
reinforcements? No."

"Oh, the shame of it," cried Cyndi, wringing her
hands in mock despair.

Katie glowered. "Then for Regionals," she went
on. "I forgot the panties that matched my practice skirt. Guess who ended up skating in a green
skirt with hot pink underwear?" She folded her
arms across her chest defiantly. "I'm not going to
forget a *thing* for Easterns. Even if it means pack-
ing up every last item I own."

On the far side of the room, Michaela Frankel
locked her own lightly packed bag with a click. "I

have packed up every last item *I* own," she announced, tossing her tawny hair behind her slight shoulders. "Except for my sadness." Her hazel eyes glowed with affection. "I will miss my roommates. My first American friends."

"Well, it's not like you're going to Timbuktu now, is it? You're only moving to an empty room on another floor, right? We'll all be here whenever you want to visit," Whitney pointed out.

"Yeah, well. I think Michaela's moving a little further away than that," hinted Cyndi, a dangerous glint in her eye.

Whitney frowned. "You'll be moving in with your aunt, then?"

"No, no. You do not understand," explained Michaela, gathering up the stray skating equipment she had stowed beneath the rollaway bed. "My aunt will be staying here in Lake Placid. But I am going on to Colorado Springs, where I will begin training next week...."

"Colorado Springs! Why, that's three-quarters of the way across the country!" Whitney exclaimed happily. "And you'll begin training there ..."

"Next week," Michaela repeated. "Just as soon as my partner arrives."

"And who *is* your new partner?" asked Katie.

"Yeah—who *is* the lucky guy?" repeated Whitney, her heart dropping to her knees. "I mean, to get such an accomplished partner as you."

The lithe foreigner waved her hands helplessly. "This, I am afraid, I cannot reveal. Even to my closest friends." Perching on her upright suitcase, she sighed heavily. "His ... how do you say, *current* affiliations do not allow for such talk. And the skating world is such a gossipy little place, no?"

"No!" shrieked Whitney, leaping from her chair as if it had been hot-wired with her in it.

"Well, you can at least tell us whether he's an American? Or someone you might have skated with before?" Claire broke in.

Whitney froze.

"Yeah, you can tell us *that* much, can't you?" Katie chimed in. "I mean, I'm a pairs skater, and I haven't heard of any potential partners on the loose—at least, not since before Regionals."

Michaela's smile was infuriatingly enigmatic. "He will be an American. And yes, we have taken to the ice together many times before. But more I simply cannot say."

"No, what more *can* you say?" Whitney whispered, pacing the room like a directionless ghost. "You've said it all already."

Cyndi tore the paper wrapper from a chocolate bar. "What? What did she say? Why am I always missing everything?"

"The sound of crunching peanuts echoing in your ears might have something to do with it," retorted Katie.

Whitney felt her face flame with fury. "She's not only stealing my partner, she's taking him halfway across the country!" She wheeled on the shocked East German girl in anger. "Admit it, Michaela! You just gave us all the details—except for Brent's name and social security number! We're not stupid, you know."

"Of course you aren't stupid," countered Michaela, rising to her own defense. "'But you *are* mistaken. You are my friend, Whitney! You have given your room to me ..."

"And now my partner," huffed Whitney. "But I didn't give him to you, did I? You just took him."

Cyndi and Claire looked to each other in dumbfounded silence, but Katie spoke up immediately.

"I don't know, Whitney—I think you might have *really* gone off the deep end this time. To think that Brent would break up with you two days before Easterns. . . . No way!"

"But that's exactly what he did—tonight in the dance studio!" Whitney slumped down onto the green carpet. "He kissed me good-bye, and said that whatever happened, he would always think of me as his partner." She rubbed away an angry tear that was welling in the corner of her eye. "It was as if he *knew* that something was about to happen. As if his bags were already packed and his taxi to the airport was waiting at the curb."

"He *kissed* you, huh?" asked Cyndi in amazement. Whitney shook her head miserably.

"But wait," Michaela began, "you do not understand—"

"Michaela, Mr. O'Casey's here to take you to the airport," called Mrs. McGregor through the door. "Say your good-byes and let's get you two on the road. Lord knows, that rattletrap truck of his already has one wheel in the grave."

While the East German girl made her rounds, kissing first Katie, then Cyndi and Claire, soundly on each cheek, Whitney seethed silently in the corner.

"I hope that you do well at your competitions, Whitney," Michaela offered. "First place at Easterns, ja?"

"I won't make your partner-to-be look bad, if that's what you mean," Whitney scoffed in response.

Michaela took her by the hand. "Soon you will understand *everything*. This I promise."

"Understand?" Whitney sounded harsh, even to herself. "Believe me, Michaela, I understand completely."

But it wasn't until the pretty East German reached out to kiss her, European-style, on both cheeks, that Whitney realized just how helpless she really felt. For in saying good-bye to Michaela Frankel, she was really saying good-bye to Brent as well.

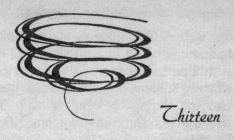

Thirteen

"*What do* you mean, you think they're *lonely*?" Clasping the beige trimline phone tightly to her ear, Katie covered the other with the fingers of her left hand.

"Oh, they won't eat," she said, glancing across the University of Rhode Island dormitory room that had been assigned to her and Whitney for the duration of the pairs and ice dancing segments of the Eastern competitions. "Did you try the shrimp, then? I think you'll have to grind them up for them. Veins and all."

Slipping her sequined, midnight-blue skating dress onto a hanger, Whitney suppressed an urge to gag. Where would Katie be calling only minutes after the pairs short program except *home*?

She sighed, feeling lonely and miserable. Not only had she avoided any possibility of conversation with Brent throughout their final practice sessions with Elena Ott, she had also managed to ice him out during the lengthy train trip that had transported the skaters from Lake Placid to Providence.

Brushing the wrinkles from the beaded blue-and-magenta skirt of her costume, Whitney tuned into the details of Katie's conversation. After worrying all morning about the upcoming Original Set Pattern ice dancing round, it was a welcome distraction.

"You took them for a *walk*? And now they're chapped? Oh, for Pete's sake." Katie stretched the telephone cord impatiently. "Well, you should have known better than to expose them to dry November air. Now you'll have to rub them down with something."

Who was Katie talking to? And what *was* the girl talking about? Her mouth suddenly as dry as the Rhode Island landscape, Whitney searched her purse for a piece of chewing gum—her only nutrition in the last two days.

"Massage them with something really thick and gooey," suggested Katie, twirling the phone cord into a long, springy spiral.

Finally a broad grin crossed the girl's face. "Yeah—*that* ought to do it? What? The competitions? Well, Tom and I are second after the short program. And Whitney and Brent ..." She cupped her hand to the receiver and whispered, still loudly enough for her roommate to hear. "Three major slips in three laps of the rink in the compulsory dances. What does *that* tell you?"

Hoisting her skates onto her blue-jeaned lap, Whitney wiped violently at the ugly scuffs and gashes they had suffered earlier that morning. Katie was right—she and Brent had accumulated as many errors as they had completed passes of the rink. She and Brent had only one thing in common now, their mutual disinterest in this competition. And while three errors in three laps was hardly the kind of average a well-established ice dance couple could welcome, they did have something to be thankful for: the exacting compulsory dance round that made up thirty percent of their overall scores hadn't been *four* laps instead of three.

Laying the receiver gently on its cradle, Katie flung her exhausted body the length of her twin bed.

"There's no problem at home, is there?" asked Whitney. "Are your parents feeling lonely with you and Tom in Lake Placid? It isn't really uncommon for . . ."

"My *parents*?" Katie howled with laughter. "I wasn't calling home, I was calling Lake Placid! For crying out loud, Whitney—that was Cyndi on the phone!"

Whitney stared blankly at her roommate.

"I was talking about the newts, you dummy!" screamed Katie. "They lost their appetite!" Sobering, she rolled onto her side and propped a pillow under her head. "Who can blame them, really? The way they've been neglected. . . ."

Whitney bristled at Katie's offhand barb. "Look, I told you I'd work on that stupid paper, and I will. It's just that I have other things on my mind right now."

"Like what? Not your skating, certainly. Three mistakes in three rounds of the rink! Really, Whitney. I'm glad I didn't have to see Elena Ott's face—or Coach Mastroni's!"

"Well, Brent had something to do with the mistakes, too," huffed Whitney. "You know, two to tango and all that."

"Well, maybe that was part of the problem—considering you guys were supposed to be skating a rhumba." Leaning on one arm, Katie watched as her angry roommate rolled the blue-sequined costume into a large, crumpled ball and shoved it into her skating bag. "Where are you going?"

Whitney pulled a thick, cable-knit sweater over her striped cotton turtleneck and threw the canvas carryall over her shoulder. "I'm going to the rink where I will make an honest attempt at the next part of this competition."

Katie rolled neatly off the edge of the bed and onto her feet. "Promise me one thing, okay?" she asked kindly, giving her roommate a fast hug.

"What's that?"

"No Backman Butt Slides this afternoon." Her eyes danced with good-natured concern. "I know you can do it. I can feel it in my bones."

"You've got it," Whitney replied, relieved to have Katie on her side during this disastrous competition.

"By the way," she added, pausing in the door,

"What about the newts' dry skin problem? I'd hate to think they were getting wrinkled before their time."

"Oh, they'll be okay," Katie answered, her face alight with mischief. "Just as soon as Cyndi starts dousing them with Shelby's precious twenty-dollars-a-bottle moisturizer!"

At that, Whitney felt better as she headed toward the rink. Maybe there was something to this feeling-in-your-bones stuff after all.

"This is no laughing matter, Whitney," said Brent, bending down to adjust his skate lace. "We're only in fourth place so far. If it weren't for Tayback and Reynolds actually falling during their fox-trot . . ."

"Right, we'd be in fifth," said Whitney, trying to pick a stray pink sequin off her deep blue bodice. "Well, maybe we'll get lucky this time."

"Oh, really?" Brent leaned morosely over the edge of the barrier in the skaters' waiting area. "Considering the way Tayback and Reynolds are skating right now, we'll need all the luck we can get."

Whitney pursed her lips and turned her attention back to the intricate beading of her skating skirt. How she hated watching the other skaters during competition! It always made her incredibly nervous.

Still, it was difficult not to be caught up in this couple's startling comeback. Only yesterday Carolyn Tayback had locked skates with her partner's during their performance, scattering both of them across the ice like windblown flakes of snow. Yet now they were back, waltzing across the ice with seemingly unlimited energy and assurance.

"Well, it's not like this part is worth much," Whitney sighed. "The set pattern marks only make up twenty percent of our total score."

"But what is it worth to them psychologically, Whitney?" Elena Ott's reminder was cool yet sharp, like the blade of a knife. "If they can continue to skate this way through one more pattern, they will enter the free dance competition full of confidence."

"Here come the marks," noted Brent after the couple had finished to a loud round of applause. "And they're going to be high."

Quickly Elena Ott began copying the numbers from the electronic scoreboard onto her program.

"You will have to skate your best," she warned, chewing on the end of her pencil as the announcer finished reading the marks. "That is all there is to it." Turning toward Whitney, she tucked a flyaway strand of golden brown hair back into her tight chignon. "You are ready then?"

Whitney nodded numbly.

"And you?" The coach brushed the padded shoulders of Brent's suit.

"As ready as I'll ever be, I guess."

"Then *skate* as if you are ready," Elena Ott urged. "As if you are ready to *win*."

Inching out onto the ice, Whitney and Brent skated very slowly along the barrier, waiting for their names to be announced.

"Let's try to correct that shoot-the-duck move,

okay?" Brent threw an arm around his partner's shoulders. "The last time I reached down to grab you . . ."

"I wasn't there?" finished Whitney angrily, shaking free of his grip. "Well, that's something you're going to have to get used to, isn't it?"

As their names and club affiliation came over the arena loudspeaker, Whitney donned the smile that had practically become a part of her costume. They made their way out to center ice.

Whitney felt Brent relax a bit as the first notes of their waltz music began. She leaned back against his chest in their opening pose, wishing their performance could already be over and done with. In a few more bars they were off. But before they had made even one complete circuit of the rink, their skates had already clashed twice. And before they could even begin the second repetition of the complicated dance choreographed for them last spring by their former coach, their tempers were clashing as well.

"You're out of position again, Whitney," Brent hissed, his teeth clenched into a furiously determined smile for the judges.

"And you're in no position to give me any grief about it," Whitney whispered back. She draped herself over her partner's arm like a wrung-out towel but beamed at the audience more brightly than the glaring arena lights.

Then, as Brent swooped her, head first, dangerously low, Whitney felt the sequined clasp that held her chignon grate against the ice. And as he propelled her back into an upright position, preparing for the swift between-the-legs pull that would usher them into the third pattern repetition, Whitney could hardly keep from gasping in shock and horror. In one brief movement her hair had come entirely undone. And though she felt the little push that sent her spiraling away from Brent like an orbiting satellite, she couldn't see his arms as they reached out to catch her. As if in slow motion, Whitney toppled toward the gouged ice.

Brent immediately picked her up, of course, and they began again from where the fall had left them, like a weary hitchhiker dumped unceremoniously onto the highway, scrambling to keep up with the ongoing waltz music. But it was no use. As far as they were concerned, this championship was over, even before the final free dance portion of the competition. There was no way they'd be able to pull up the standings now, short of a miracle—and no chance of their qualifying for the upcoming national championships.

"Well, I hope you're satisfied now, Brent Marks," Whitney sobbed, her back toward the scoreboard that, within seconds, would humiliate her completely. Wiping away a furious tear, she twisted her unkempt mass of hair back into some semblance of order. "I knew you wanted to be rid of me, but to actually throw a competition! If that's not the meanest, cruelest, most thoughtless . . ."

"Throw a competition!" Brent's face was incredulous. "You actually think I did that on purpose? Have you lost your marbles?" He pointed to the row of scores now flashing on the scoreboard. "Those are my marks, too, you know!"

"And you deserve them," said Whitney, finally daring to glance up at the surprisingly high marks—5.3s and 5.4s—that they had been awarded for technical merit. "Where were you out there, anyway? Halfway to Colorado Springs?"

Brent seemed confused but recovered quickly. "No, Whitney—the question is, where were *you*? I reached down expecting you to *be* there and instead you were sliding across the ice like some runaway hockey puck."

"I was just where you threw me," she shot back, slapping her skate guards across the palm of her hand in frustration. "As usual. I am so sick of all this."

"Here's something else that might throw you," said Gregory Mastroni, who as usual had watched the entire debacle from the shadows of the massive arena. "By some stroke of luck your artistic scores were good enough to keep you in fourth place. With a half-decent showing in the free dance round, you two might even manage to move up to third in this competition and qualify for Nationals."

"You mean we might actually end up with a *medal*?" Brent asked, watching intently as Elena Ott figured and refigured the complicated ordinals one last time.

"It's a possibility," replied Coach Mastroni, his face as impenetrable as a looming stone wall. "Who knows, maybe with another medal under your belts, both of you may find the kind of partners who can ..."

"Wait a minute," Brent interrupted, waving his skate guards as if to knock the skating school director's words right out of the air. "Are you saying that no matter how we do in this competition, we'll be getting new partners?"

"I'm saying that being at each other's throats has cheated you both out of at least one gold medal already—at Regionals." The coach stared resolutely at the skaters now taking the ice. "And considering your performance here so far ..."

"But you said we had a chance," Whitney said softly, surprised to find herself suddenly hopeful.

"You *do* have a chance—a very slim one, but a chance nonetheless."

Brent swallowed hard.

"Then what are our chances of being allowed to stay together after this competition?"

Gregory Mastroni smiled as if amused. "Roughly? About the same as the chance of snow in July. Or that Coach Ott and I will be ice dancing partners in the next Olympics." His face grew solemn again. "What I'm saying is, you two have about as much chance of skating together next season as either one of you has of actually winning this silly war you've declared on each other ... Very little chance at all."

Fourteen

Whitney, who had just spent fifteen minutes struggling into her favorite skating outfit, a deep violet dress with a petal-shaped skirt, stared at her pale reflection in the locker room mirror. Her hair was a total mess. A can of super-hold mousse in one hand, her brush poised in the other, Whitney surveyed the damage skeptically. Tease, curl, and spray as she might, her hair had never before reflected her state of mind like it did right now.

Gregory Mastroni had given Brent odds on whether Backman and Marks would still be an ice dancing team even after the Easterns were over. But why had Brent even have thought to *ask* for those odds? In a matter of days he would be meeting Michaela Frankel in Colorado Springs to begin training with a new coach. Surely there was no chance that he would back out of that arrangement to remain in Lake Placid with Whitney. *Was* there?

Whitney yanked the brush mercilessly through her hair in a halfhearted attempt at a chignon. It was insane to think that Brent would actually consider giving up a chance to skate with Michaela Frankel. Why would he choose a second-rate rhumba dropout over an international champion? She studied the brushed-out remains of what had been intended as a Grace Kelly upsweep.

"Aha—I thought I might find you in here!" Katie's cheerful voice echoed over the austere white tile.

"Wait till you hear what I have to tell you! Whitney, you won't *believe* your ears!" She came up behind her and patted her roommate's uncooperative hair. "You *do* still have ears in there somewhere, don't you?"

Whitney handed over the hairbrush and sighed. "Katie, I swear if you have come in here five minutes before my free-dance program to harrass me about this hair ..."

"No, no," Katie assured her, expertly twisting the gold-brown strands into a neat braid. "Believe me, Whitney, what I've got to say is a lot more important than that! I was on the phone with Cyndi and ..."

"And the newts are now the proud parents of oviparous quintuplets. That's just *wonderful*." Whitney flung a handful of bobby pins across the room in her fury. "Katie, I don't care about your stupid newts! Right now I've got other things on my mind. And I don't care what Cyndi had to say."

"Not even if it's something that was on the local Lake Placid news today?" Katie retrieved the bobby pins like a well-trained setter. "Not even if it has to do with Michaela Frankel?"

"Are you kidding? I don't want to hear it *especially* if it has to do with her," Whitney replied hotly. "Not now." Not minutes before a major competition that I can't hope to win, she added to herself miserably. But could any prize satisfy her after losing Brent's heart?

Giving herself a final once-over, Whitney gathered up the clutter she had scattered across the dressing table, shoved it into her canvas tote, and passed it on to Katie.

"She really did make the headlines, you know," Katie said, stuffing the bag under her arm like a football. "I mean, I really think you ought to . . ."

"And I really think you ought to butt out, Katie Arden, before the headlines read something like this." Whitney waved her arm dramatically. '"Psychotic Skater Maims Idiot Roommate with Skate Guard—Newts Mourn.'" She grinned. "Okay?"

"Okay," Katie nodded, "if that's the way you want it."

"Beautiful," commented Elena Ott, entranced by the elegant artistry of the couple now whirling across the ice. She clasped her hands as if in prayer. "Just beautiful."

"That music's going to kill them, though," Gregory Mastroni said impassively. "There's something about ice dancing to opera that doesn't play in Peoria. Or Providence, for that matter."

"Well, let's not forget, Carolyn Tayback may not have had anything to say about the music she's skating to," said Whitney, giving her partner a sidelong glance. "Heaven knows, the Beatles weren't my choice."

Brent rolled his eyes. "I wouldn't complain about the Beatles if I were you. 'The Long and Winding Road' took us all the way to Lake Placid, didn't it?"

"Sure," Whitney replied. "And now 'Something' is taking *you* all the way to Colorado Springs. Or should I say *somebody*?"

"Does *anybody* have any idea what Whitney's talking about?" Gregory Mastroni asked wearily.

Brent shrugged. "I don't."

"Nor I," added Elena Ott.

"Look," said Whitney, putting her hands on her hips. "It's no secret that Brent is going off to train in Colorado." Why was everyone going to such lengths to hide that fact from her? Were they just waiting until after the competition was over to break the news?

Brent's jaw dropped. "That's ridiculous," he scoffed.

"That's *crazy*," added Coach Mastroni. "He's enrolled at Lake Placid until June."

"It is *not* crazy," Whitney insisted. "It's the truth, admit it! Backman and Marks are being disbanded as a team so that Brent here can perform his

precious Frankel Twist with the genuine article—
Michaela Frankel."

"Insane," pronounced Mastroni.

"In your dreams," added Elena Ott, demonstrating everything she knew about American slang.
"Michaela's partner has only today arrived in Colorado Springs. And he is certainly not Brent Marks.
His build is all wrong for my niece."

"Though I *could* have a growth spurt," Brent
teased.

Ignoring him, Whitney spun to face her East
German coach. "Then who *is* Michaela's new
partner?"

"Why, Andreas Licht, of course. She has skated
with him since they were babies." Elena Ott
smoothed the sides of Whitney's backswept braid.
"And you see why she could not warn you. Defection is a somewhat dangerous matter."

Whitney could not have felt more confused and
embarrassed than if she had been the butt of
some cruel joke. Was *this* what Katie had been
trying to tell her back in the locker room? Still,
disbelief nagged at her like a chronic headache.

"But Michaela said her new partner would be
American!" she said, frowning.

"Andy *will* be an American. And so will Michaela
and I, as soon as the matter is settled with the
good people at immigration."

"Then what about this mysterious 'current affiliation'?" Whitney persisted. "Andy Licht wasn't
skating with anyone else, right?"

"There you are quite correct," Elena replied. "I
think perhaps my niece meant the tie between
her partner and his country."

Brent cleared his throat loudly.

"Then, I guess that makes me ... wrong," said Whitney slowly. She rubbed her sticky palms briskly against the front of her skating dress. What was it about making apologies that was so difficult for her?

"Not only that, but these marks put you in fifth place, behind Tayback and Reynolds," noted Gregory Mastroni, examining the scores over Elena Ott's shoulder. "You'll have to really pull it out in the free dance."

"Now?" Whitney stared blankly at the second set of marks for Tayback and Reynolds, then back at her partner. "We can't possibly skate now! Oh, Brent—there's so much I have to say to you! I was wrong—about you, about Michaela, and even about my own feelings...."

Gregory Mastroni coughed loudly. "Look, you two, you've got about three seconds to get out onto that ice."

"And about four-and-one-half minutes to prove that *I* was wrong," added Elena Ott. She smiled thinly. "Coach Mastroni may occasionally select fifth-place skaters, but I do not. For me, it is champions only."

Brent extended his hand to Whitney. "Well, what do you say? Can we get through this without kissing the boards?"

In answer, Whitney boosted herself up on the tips of her toe picks and brushed her lips gently against Brent's cheek.

A few glorious minutes later, it was all over—almost.

"Only a 5.7 from judge number three?" complained Whitney, peering at the seven people seated at the judges' table, while Brent surveyed their high technical merit scores with pride. "Why, that was a near-perfect performance."

Brent's eyes were shining with mischief. "It could have been perfect if it hadn't been for that botched Frankel Twist. Where were you on that landing, anyway?"

Whitney responded in an exaggerated Southern-belle drawl. "Why, ah was tryin' to avoid those freezin' cold hands of yours, Brent Marks. Lord knows y'all couldn't catch a cold in a wind tunnel."

Wrapping his arms possessively around his partner's waist, Brent whispered softly in her ear, "You know how the saying goes, Whitney: 'Cold hands, warm heart.'"

She smiled and leaned back further into the warmth of his strong embrace. "There's another old saying that might be of interest to you, Mr. Marks."

"And what that might be?"

Whitney tipped her face up to his. "Kiss your partner and you'll kiss the boards."

"What do you say we tempt the fates?" Brent said with a grin. He turned Whitney toward him as smoothly as he had on the ice and cupped her chin in his large, smooth hands. "Tonight? After dinner?"

"Artistic impression scores, coming up," interrupted Elena Ott. The marks appeared on the electronic scoreboard almost instantly. "Yes, it is ours! The silver is ours!"

"Hey, what do you know?" said Brent, whirling Whitney excitedly in his arms. "I have a date with an Eastern ice dance silver medalist!"

"That's where you're wrong," corrected Whitney. "I'm the one who has a date with the real star of this competition."

"That's where you're *both* wrong," declared Katie Arden, gleefully leaping down from the stands behind them.

Whitney and Brent only stared at her.

"Medals or no medals, you've *both* got dates— with a starving, grossly neglected pair of newts! And I'm going to see that you keep those dates if I have to drag you, skates and all!"

"Okay, Katie, we give up!" replied Brent with a laugh, his hands above his head in mock surrender. "We'll give the newts their due. We promise." He turned to Whitney. "Who knows? We might even learn something."

"About *amphibians*?" Whitney asked in disbelief.

"No, Whitney, about us," whispered Brent, wrapping her in his arms.

She sighed deeply. "Now that's a subject that might be worth researching."

"And I know just where to start," he said, and he lowered his lips to meet hers in a long, lingering kiss.

Here's a look at what's ahead in FACE THE MUSIC, the third book in Fawcett's "Silver Skates" series for GIRLS ONLY.

"It's so good to see you, Cynthia," said Miriam Mireau-Scott, giving her daughter a peck on each cheek. "Though I can't say you're looking particularly well."

"And it's nice to see you, too, Mother," Cyndi answered stiffly. "As always."

The chic brunette woman shrugged out of her fur coat and adjusted the collar of her blue wool suit. Then she surveyed Cyndi and shook her head. "Well, just *look* at you, Cynthia!" The ex-ballerina threw up one hand in frustration. "Surely you never looked as ... *unkempt* as this at home."

Cyndi stared down at the floor.

Mimi settled onto the nearest chair as lightly as a bird upon its perch. "Here we are, then."

"Mother, why are you here?" Poised on the edge of Claire's lower bunk, Cyndi pulled a pillow onto her lap as if to camouflage any telltale bulges. "I know you've been to school to see the principal—"

"In whose estimation you have *not* been working to potential," replied the woman, twirling one lapiz earring.

"And I heard that you've been talking with Coach Mastroni—"

"You heard about a meeting you could not have *seen* since you very rarely appear at the rink," commented the ballerina, spreading the sable across her lap. "Not that you have much to practice for, as I understand it."

Cyndi swallowed hard. So, Mastroni had spilled the beans about her dismal competitive year—and the devastating losses that had excluded her from the

Eastern and National competitions. And why not? Her mother and the Ice Man were two of a kind—generous in their demands and infuriatingly skimpy with their praise.

"Okay, so you've heard the bad news," Cyndi acknowledged. "But after all, I'm only fifteen—"

"*Only* fifteen?" The dancer's brows arched. "Do I really need to remind you, my dear, that at the ripe old age of twelve I had already been accepted at the Royal Ballet School in London? And that when I was fifteen, practicing seven or eight hours a day, I weighed only eighty-nine pounds?"

Cyndi looked guiltily up at the ceiling. "Mother, please!"

"The fact is, Cynthia," Mimi Mireau continued, "you don't seem to be making it here at the Lake Placid Skating School. Your competition performances haven't been up to your potential. You haven't even been showing up for practice." The genteel dancer tapped her lower lip. "And then again, there's the problem of your weight."

"So what do you want me to do, Mother?" Cyndi asked.

"What I want you to do, Cynthia, is to get your act together—to show some progress with your appearance as well as your skating. You will feel much better about yourself, I assure you. I want you to prove that you belong here in Lake Placid ... by the time of the Christmas show."

"But that's only three weeks away," Cyndi protested, close to tears.

Her mother stood up. "Cynthia, you have been in Lake Placid for three months now. An additional three weeks seems plenty of time to decide whether you want to stay here—or whether you would be better off at home in Illinois."

Barbara J. Mumma has long been captivated by the glamorous, fiercely competitive world of amateur figure skating. Her passion for the beauty and grace of on-ice performance took her behind the scenes as well, offering her a first-hand glimpse of the less-than-glitzy side of athletic artistry: from the pressures of rigorous training to the trauma of injury; from the personal costs of no-holds-barred competition to the disappointment of defeat. A longtime book editor, she is the author of several young adult and adult books.

GIRLS ONLY

SATIN SLIPPERS

The Lure of the Stage...
The Thrill of the Applause!

An exciting new GIRLS ONLY series that sweeps young readers into the heart and soul of ballet—from the glamour and romance of the stage to the incredible discipline, strength, and sacrifice required to get there.

Leah Stephenson, our young heroine, has studied ballet since she was four, and now at fifteen auditions for the San Francisco Ballet Academy. Thus begins her adventures as she performs for an audience for the first time, experiences jealousy and competition from the other dancers, and at the same time deals with her family, friends and school.